Two Lines

World Writing in Translation

Issue 28, Spring 2018

Two Lines Press

EDITOR

CJ Evans

MANAGING EDITOR

Jessica Sevey

SENIOR EDITORS

Scott Esposito

Michael Holtmann

ASSOCIATE EDITOR

Emily Wolahan

EDITORIAL ASSISTANT

Sarah Coolidge

FOUNDING EDITOR

Olivia Sears

DESIGN

Isabel Urbina Peña

COVER DESIGN

Quemadura

SUBSCRIPTIONS

Two Lines is published twice annually.
Subscriptions are $15 per year; individual
issues are $12. To subscribe, visit:
www.twolinespress.com

BOOKSTORES

Two Lines is distributed by
Publishers Group West. To order,
call: 1-800-788-3123

TWO LINES

Issue 28

ISBN 978-1-931883-69-6

ISSN 1525-5204

© 2018 by Two Lines Press

582 Market Street, Suite 700

San Francisco, CA 94104

www.twolinespress.com

twolines@catranslation.org

This project is supported in part by an award
from the National Endowment for the Arts.

ART WORKS.
arts.gov

Editor's Note

Last week Spotify sent me a playlist, and I love probably ninety-nine percent of the songs on it. I was also looking for a new kitchen faucet online, and now every ad I see is for a faucet I'd probably buy. But I hate shopping for anything, let alone faucets. And, even though I love each song, the Spotify playlist tailored just for me is a horrible mix that mashes my workout music against music I listen to just before bed.

Not everything in this issue of *Two Lines* was chosen just for you, but each was chosen lovingly, and I'd suspect some of the things you'll like best will be surprises, which don't fit neatly into what you'd *be expected* to like. Literature is a place where an individual, half a world away, can say something unique to them and you immediately feel it, despite never having thought of it in that way, like the frustration of being a kid in Saskia Vogel's translation from Johanne Lykke Holm's *The Night before This Day*:

> It's a terrible thing to be a child. You stand in line with the animals, the crops, and the machines. You open your mouth and speak. You hear the adults say: *Something's coming out of that child-mouth. Impossible to know what.*

Or the loneliness of the angel in "Mirror" by Carsten René Nielsen, translated by David Keplinger: "...an angel, who is giving itself a shave. Even though it has no reflection, it holds up a shaving mirror and lifts up the chin, as it has seen humans do."

Literature is the wonder that comes from learning that you already know something incredibly personal to someone you'll never meet, from somewhere you had never considered and no algorithm could have possibly guessed.

CJ EVANS

Fiction

Poetry

Essay

FRANCESCO PICCOLO , author and screenwriter, writes for *Corriere della Sera*, one of Italy's leading newspapers. He is a lead screenwriter of the HBO TV series based on Elena Ferrante's best-selling novel *My Brilliant Friend*. His novel *Il desiderio di essere come tutti* was awarded the prestigious Strega Prize.

Il desiderio di essere come tutti

Sono nato in un giorno di inizio estate del 1973, a nove anni.

Fino a quel momento la mia vita, e tutti i fatti che accadevano nel mondo, erano due entità separate, che non potevano incontrarsi in nessun modo. Me ne stavo nella mia casa, nel mio cortile, nella mia città; con i miei genitori, i miei fratelli, i compagni di scuola, i parenti e gli amici—e in un altro pianeta accadevano i fatti che guardavo in televisione. Ogni tanto i grandi ne parlavano, del mondo e dell'Italia in particolare; quindi c'era interesse verso quello che accadeva al di fuori della nostra vita. Ma noi tutti, in ogni caso, non c'entravamo niente. E io, ancora meno.

ERA APPENA FINITA la scuola. Massimo, il mio compagno di banco, mi invitava il pomeriggio a giocare da lui. Era molto ricco, aveva una villa gigantesca a Briano. Aveva appena conosciuto un ragazzino del paese, basso, con tante lentiggini e pochi capelli; non sapeva stare fermo, parlava soltanto in dialetto, e ci sembrava che sapesse tutto di ogni cosa come se fosse un adulto dentro il corpo di un ragazzino. Noi stavamo zitti, lo ascoltavamo e poi facevamo quello che faceva lui. Disse che ci avrebbe portato in un posto segreto, se avevamo il coraggio. Noi dicemmo subito di sí, anche se avevamo paura. Ci vedemmo il giorno dopo, era tardi, ma il sole non calava mai, e il . . .

Wanna Be Like Everyone

I was born one day in the early summer of 1973, at the age of nine.

Until that moment, my life, and all the things that happened out in the world, were two separate entities that simply had no way of intersecting. I stayed safe at home in my family's apartment, in my courtyard, in my city; with my parents, my brothers and sisters, the kids from school, relatives, and friends—and the events that I saw on television instead occurred on some distant planet. Every so often the grown-ups did talk about those events, about the world, and about Italy in particular; that meant we took some interest in what happened outside our own life. Still, none of us had anything to do with it. Me, least of all.

SCHOOL HAD JUST LET OUT for the summer. Massimo, who sat next to me in class, invited me over to his house to play in the afternoons. He was very rich; he had a gigantic villa in Briano. He had just met a kid from the town of Briano, who was short and had lots of freckles and not much hair; this kid couldn't sit still, spoke only in dialect, and seemed to know all about everything in great detail, as if he were a grown-up in the body of a little kid. Massimo and I kept our mouths shut, listened to him, and then did whatever he was doing. He told us he'd take us to a secret place, if we had the courage to come along. We immediately said yes, though we were actually scared. We met up the next day and, even though it was already late, the sun just wouldn't set, and the freckle-faced kid told us to follow him. We went through the woods; he knew exactly where to go and how to get there. He'd done this lots of times before, he said. And he told us that we were not to say a word to anyone else about it. We swore we wouldn't, and asked no questions.

Our path ended at a wall. Fairly high, but not *too* high. Just a little farther, he said a couple of times, and led the way. We walked along, our shoulders brushing against the wall. Then we came to a place where he said: Here. He wedged his foot into a little nook that he knew about, hoisted himself up, grabbed the edge of the wall, and pulled himself up to the top. Just do like me, he said. Then he jumped down the other side, vanishing from sight. Massimo did exactly the same thing.

Now it was my turn. Over on the other side, Massimo was calling to me: Come on, jump up. Over on this side, I was afraid I wouldn't be able to. I grabbed the wall, lifted my leg, looking for a foothold that would support me, and then pulled myself up, expending much greater effort than I'd seen either of them require; then, pressing my whole torso against the edge, I hauled myself up to the top of the wall. And then I jumped down. There was no longer anyone there waiting for me. I was still surrounded by trees, but now I was on the far side of the wall, where the light streamed down strong and bright: but the trees, I realized, were few and far between. Just beyond the trees, I saw the two of them, standing still and looking around.

So I, too, came forth into the light.

OF COURSE, I HAD REALIZED right away that this wall was the wall that ran around the Palace. We all knew, in Caserta, that the Palace started in the center of town and climbed up the side of the hills. But I'd never calculated the perimeter of the interior as related to the size of the exterior. That is to say, when the freckle-faced kid had said: Here—I couldn't size up where we actually were.

So I was struck breathless.

We were up high, near the top, just below the waterfall, up where anyone would want to climb to when they entered the Palace. I walked along slowly, with one hand skimming atop the surface of the water just over the rim of the great fountain, my eyes drawn by the statue of a half-naked woman who was covered by a fluttering cloth, a cloth that concealed the parts of her you weren't supposed to see. Around her stood a number of other distraught women; they too were half naked. On the opposite side was a stag surrounded by dogs, dogs that seemed distinctly ill-intentioned. I cared little about the stag, much more about the woman.

The truly unbelievable thing, though, was that there was no one else in sight. The Palace had closed for the day, everyone had left, and the kid with the freckles actually claimed that at this moment, inside these walls, throughout the palace grounds, in the woods, the English garden, and the royal apartments, there was no one but the three of us. This state of affairs, however, didn't strike him as particulary noteworthy. He was just telling us this to reassure us about the refrigerator.

THE SUN HAD SET SOME TIME BEFORE, evening was falling very gradually, and there was still some daylight, that barely luminous kind of daylight, stunning and lovely. Massimo and the freckle-faced kid had gone straight to where he'd meant to take us: in a corner there stood an enormous refrigerator, with a lock and chain that our freckled friend had learned to open with great ease. And inside it were chocolate-nut ice cream cones, Cokes, orangeades, mineral waters—anything you could possibly want.

There was that refrigerator, and this was the secret we were sworn not to reveal. And there was the Palace, completely empty, but we hadn't come here for the Palace. If the other two kept quiet—when they did finally keep quiet, in a pause amid all their excitement—you could clearly hear the slow, faint sound of the water in the waterfall, which was a very gentle waterfall. A sound that I had never before perceived so distinctly. The statues of the woman and her girlfriends, of the stag and of the dogs, were there, more motionless and more speechless, alone. All the other times I'd been up here before—so many times, especially on Sundays, or when some relative or friend from out of town came to visit, we had climbed all the way up here, which was where the tours ended, the highest point (you weren't allowed to climb up from here onto the rocks of the waterfall), the most beautiful spot in the Palace—there was always a huge crowd of people milling around the rim of the basin, pointing at the stag and explaining how he had been transformed into a stag in the first place, and why the woman was covering

Translated by Antony Shugaar • Italian | Italy

herself so modestly. There were children sticking their hands into the water (as I'd done myself just a moment ago), horse-drawn carriages, and buses that pulled up, unloaded more visitors, and then pulled away.

But right here and right now, in the Palace, there really was no one else.

I positioned myself with a bottle of cold Coca-Cola at the center of the clearing, sitting on the rim of the fountain, and turned my back on the woman and the stag. Massimo and the other kid were kicking up a fuss, fooling around with the refrigerator and the ice cream cones, then they'd vanish into the trees; they were keyed up, they kept coming back, running over and sticking their heads into the refrigerator again. Then, after taking all the stuff they could carry, they said: Let's go. I said, Sure. Out of the corner of my eye I waited for them to jump over to the other side of the wall, while Massimo said: Come on, hurry up.

It's not as if I wasn't afraid; I was definitely very much afraid to be left alone there, even if only for a moment. But the truth is that I wanted to do this, and I wanted to so very much that I thought a little less of the fear: I wanted to stay here all alone, in the Palace, perhaps entirely alone in the whole Palace, even if only for thirty seconds. I had no idea why I wanted to, but I could sense with great precision that I did.

I had the sensation that I was no longer inside this enormous and familiar thing that stood across from my house...

They climbed over the wall, it never even occurred to them that I wasn't following them, so they raised no objections, and maybe they started walking away. I just stood there, with my back to the fountain and ahead of me, the immensely long expanse of the park, all those basins running downhill, the Palace itself at the bottom, and the trees marking the edges of the woods along both sides.

I had the feeling, in that instant, in a silence unlike anything I've ever heard since—a silence made up of the water from the falls—that I was inside something gigantic, something that couldn't have been conceived merely as a way of letting us steal ice cream from the refrigerator, couldn't have been conceived just for us three who lived here in this moment. I lived in an apartment house, down there on the left, not far from the opposite wall, and every time I looked out my window at home I saw a side of the Palace. And

I really didn't care all that much about it. I was born here, this was my life, it had just happened that way, it was neither my doing nor was it my fault, this enormous thing had always stood next to my house, as long as I'd been in existence, and I went there on Sundays the same way people in any city seek out the nearest park to get themselves a little fresh air.

And yet, for those seconds, it seemed to me that all this came from a long way off, and that it had a history; and above all, that it didn't concern us alone, just my family, Massimo, and that other kid, the refrigerator that we'd broken into, my city, and the people that I knew there. I had the sensation that I was no longer inside this enormous and familiar thing that stood across from my house, but instead that I was inside something else, less easy to identify within the context of my everyday existence, but more recognizable in absolute terms. Practically speaking, for an instant there entered into my head an intuition that matched that solitude and yet, at the same time, negated it: at the very moment that I *was* alone in the world, I started to notice that I wasn't alone in the world. It seemed to me, for one hallucinatory instant, that all the walkways and all the grounds were completely overrun by hundreds of thousands of people, millions of them, walking from the suites of the Palace uphill toward the waterfall, and that these were all the human beings that had ever set foot in the Palace from the day it had been built until this very afternoon. And I was there too, in their midst.

This sensation of being part of the world, for a few seconds, made me euphoric and frightened, every bit as euphoric and frightened as I was to have been left alone in here. But I wasn't able to grasp the essence of what was happening to me: or actually, I think that I did understand it—or perhaps I should say: sensed it—for an instant, and then just as quickly it vanished. It struck me suddenly that the daylight had faded to darkness; and so I whipped around, as if trying to run away, and jumped over the wall, with effort but energy, because I wanted to get to the other side, back to where Massimo and that kid were now, but especially because I wanted to get back into my life, the one I knew and that didn't scare me—a life that might not fill me with euphoria, but that didn't frighten me, either.

And in fact, in the time it took me to fall back over to this side of the wall, I had already lost the sensation of being part of the world, and it now seemed like a transitory and insignificant thing. I set foot back in the life I'd been living until that moment, and all those thoughts disappeared. In

Translated by Antony Shugaar • Italian | Italy

part because I had to run and catch up with those others: it was already too dark to see a thing anymore.

THEN ALL OF THAT SUDDENLY vanished on the morning of March 16.

That sensation of the world ending was such a commonly and widely experienced sensation that now it hardly even bears mentioning. For a few hours, there was a general notion that something far more deadly serious than what had just happened on Via Fani was about to befall us all. As if this was just the beginning of who knows what else.

The morning that Aldo Moro was kidnapped, personal life and public life stopped being two separate things. This time it wasn't just in one part of the country, the way it had been with the cholera outbreak; now it was in every single human being. One of those happenings that for the rest of your life you tell people where you were, what you were doing. That morning no Italian would have been able to withdraw his or her own individual existence from its part in the larger community. That day everyone, even the most blithely indifferent, was forced to be born for the second time.

What happened to me was my definitive loss of innocence. It had never occurred to me that the life I thought could be lived between the courtyard and the country at large, the life that I knew was also steeped in violence somewhere else, could possibly be struck by such a gigantic act of war. Like all kids—who imagine the world without even considering the present, thinking only of the future, which they imagine to be pretty much irresistible—I had the clear perception that all the horror in the world had already taken place, that it formed part of the past. And everything that happened now, in my present day, was part of a progressive abandonment of the most lacerating and ravaging historical events. Even the cholera outbreak, which had occurred so close by, hadn't after all had either lasting nor devastating effects. For that matter, so far even the terrorist attacks seemed to have little to do with a boy in Caserta who was trying to find some way to imagine life; I had managed to convince myself that these were just remnants of the past, rather than a bellwether of any future that might be taking form here and now. From this moment on, I was no longer authorized to look at the world from below, and go on saying that after all, even if I'd already been born a second time, deep down, I had nothing to do with it. The Moro kidnapping, that military operation which had killed men who now lay facedown in their own blood, hanging half out of a car, those ponderous, sorrowful voices of commentators speaking live about things they were still unable to grasp, and therefore conveying a sense of astounded terror that just made the fear worse, a fear that took a long, long time to go away—all this was final and definitive proof that I too, like everybody else, was part of the larger community.

Because that kidnapping really was the exact point where a man's life intersected with the life of a community. It was the kidnapping of a statesman but also of a human being. It was the kidnapping of a representative of the community at large, but also of a man with a family. A matter that was by no means relegated to the background in the events that followed: in fact, while we all felt ourselves drawn deep, in the very core of our lives, into the heart of community, the chairman of the Christian Democratic Party, the person who most fully embodied the political strategies of those years and, especially, of those days, drew a curtain—who knows at what precise instant during those hours—across his public life, deciding that above all else, he was the father of a family, a fact that had never even occurred to any of us. That was the moment when we discovered that Moro—and at that point, also all the others—had a family and a life outside of the one that we could see.

WHEN THE CLASSROOM DOOR flew open and we were told to hurry outside because the Red Brigades had kidnapped Aldo Moro and there was a curfew in place, we all stood up in silence, and there was only the sound of the chairs and the desks. We were all stunned, and ready to be terrified. Or actually, I ought to say, not all of us.

I was a freshman in science high school. I sat next to a girl named Elena. Maybe I wasn't in love with her yet, or maybe I was but hadn't admitted it to myself, or maybe I was but I just hadn't realized it yet. She was a girl my age, but she might as well have been ten years older. She belonged to the Movement, she and her boyfriend. Her family and her boyfriend's family were all Communists. She and her boyfriend (that's not the word we used, it was a ridiculous word, this much I can remember clearly; but what I can't remember is what word we used instead) were Communists in a much more extreme way. And while the rest of us were all getting up wordlessly and doing our best to get home as quickly as possible, which seemed like the only sensible thing to do, I looked over at her—I was always looking over at her, I think—and I saw that her eyes were laughing. She was contented. She was taking her time getting ready to leave. She was relaxed, not frightened in the slightest, not unhappy in the slightest. She too looked at me, for a second, and in a small voice, confident and fierce, told me: "The revolution has begun."

In the face of this unmistakable force of hers, it was now my turn to decide. Whether I ought to hold deep inside me the terror that had washed over me, or else to put a secret smile at the corner of my mouth, showing her that I favored the beginning of the revolution. I wished I could please her then and there by displaying the nerve and courage appropriate to the moment, but also—thinking back on it now, in hindsight—a very considerable cynicism (which I could see in her eyes). But I just didn't have it in me. I turned and headed after the others as they ran. She, however, started running too, along with the rest of us. But the way she ran was different from the way we did.

> I watched them, I envied them; and at the same time, my stomach ached with nausea.

Once we were outside, we all headed for home, as we'd been told to do. All of us, that is, except for the kids in the Movement. Elena hung back with them. As I hurried out the front gate and went practically galloping the length of the school's green metal fence, I saw that Elena and those others were hugging. You couldn't say they were happy, considering that an unmistakable terror was painted on their faces too, but they knew, and conveyed to each other—here was the meaning of those hugs—that they weren't a bit sorry that the Red Brigades had kidnapped Moro.

I stopped to watch them for a moment, hanging on the bars of the fence. I looked at Elena with her comrades; and I looked at the others running away just as I was. How very different from the world I wanted to belong to, how very similar to the rest of the world to which I *did* belong, whether or not I wanted to. I felt pain and sorrow bearing in on me from all directions, from Moro's side, from the side of all those who, like me, were hurrying home, and I felt sorrow that I was not complicit with the very ones I wanted to be like, sorrow that it hadn't occurred to me that the revolution had just begun, and sorrow for the fact that all I felt, now that it *had* begun, was terror, alienation, and cowardice; and an even noisier, subterranean sorrow that, despite the fact that I wanted to be like them, what they were doing was so alien to me, it was a symptom of such violence, that there was no way I could view it as acceptable. I watched them, I envied them; and at the same time, my stomach ached with nausea.

A great many people acted pleased, at least right then and there. Then, later, as time passed, they censored that reaction. But I saw that Elena was almost overjoyed, in an awkward, inappropriate manner; a dangerous, senseless, morbid happiness. She scared me, I was afraid of her and the other kids in the Movement, and so I ran away all the faster. I wanted to be like them, with them; and had wanted it since the very first day I arrived at that high school. But now, the act of running felt right. Put quite simply, they were beaming with joy, and I felt helpless. They were courageous, and I was scared. It was now clear to me what had happened a few days earlier while reading Camilla Cederna's book: I was incapable of being the way I wanted to be.

THEN, LUCKILY, EVERYONE CAME to my rescue. They also came to the rescue—immediately, I have to say, and just in the nick of time—of a tiny thought that was about to pop up in my head, a thought that, thanks only to the sheer scope of the tragedy and the serious and nonjudgmental involvement of my father, I had so far managed to reject: namely, that if Communism really was about to arrive, as he claimed, and if it was about to arrive like this, then I truly could no longer be on that side; instead, I was on my father's side, and nearly everyone else's side. At this moment, even though I'd always thought I was different, all I wanted was to be like everyone. Like my father and my mother, like my neighbors, like the people talking on the evening news broadcast. Like Uncle Nino. And like Aunt Rosa.

Sure enough, she was the first glimmer of comfort. When I got home, she was standing on the sidewalk outside our front door: her grief and horror resembled mine, and if anything it was more conscious, determined, and indignant. And in fact, the Italian Communist Party, the labor unions, the

Translated by Antony Shugaar • Italian | Italy

people who were immediately demonstrating in the streets, all of them came hurrying to my rescue as I struggled in my alienation. Now, every time I see pictures of that piazza—of those piazzas—filled with people, I am stirred almost to tears: both because it's one of those moments when you can clearly see, unblurred, the country as a whole, you can see it etched out in its shape and makeup, and you can see, inside the country, all the people it contains, all the people who design it as it is and, at the same time, the way it ought to be, exactly and precisely the way you almost never (in fact, never) see it; as if those people in the streets composed in the best way possible an enormous jigsaw puzzle that finally, seen like this, makes sense. But I'm also stirred at the thought of how comforting it was, that day, not to feel estranged from what I wanted to resemble, what I wanted to be a part of.

After that, day after day, I also saw Elena's sadness grow, and her doubts grow with it. So did her fear of the things that were happening, and that strange smile of hers, luckily, went away. As time passed, I silently fell in love with her. Or realized that I already was.

ON THE EVENING OF July 9, 1994, the prime minister of Italy, Silvio Berlusconi, spent a long time admiring the fountain of Diana and Acteon in the Palace of Caserta. I can't say that the people who were with him were his friends, but he too was inside the Palace while it was closed to the public, and he hadn't even had to climb over a wall. It was already dark, but for the first time the entire park had been illuminated at night—and it was empty.

With him was his wife, Veronica, Bill and Hillary Clinton, Boris Yeltsin, François Mitterrand, John Major, and many others. That year, the meeting of the world's great powers, the G7 (to which was added Yeltsin's Russia, for a day), had been held in Naples. There had been diplomatic meetings, first ladies strolling along the waterfront esplanade and to the New Castle, the Maschio Angioino, there was an excursion down the Amalfi coast, and Bill Clinton had gone out for a pizza in the city center. For the last evening, a gala dinner had been scheduled in the banquet halls of the Palace of Caserta. People told me that there was a great deal of excitement in our city, as well as various urban improvement projects: there was special lighting in the Palace park. We had lived our whole lives with a Palace that closed before sunset, a silent and frightening darkness next to our very-much-alive houses, in the city. The evening of the gala dinner, the President of the Italian Republic, Oscar Luigi Scalfaro, welcomed the guests, who were enchanted by the Royal Palace, and then the lights went on, illuminating the whole park, all the way up to the waterfall.

AFTER DINNER, THE CARS TOOK THEM all on a long tour of the grounds, and then stopped way up high, at the fountain. Berlusconi and the other men, with their wives, got out of the cars and strolled around the fountain. A few of them even skimmed their fingers over the surface of the water. And in the midst of that cool and lovely evening, while everyone admired Diana's surprised glance and the way the dogs were tearing Acteon limb from limb, and how the waterfall gently broke through the silence, and down below them the entire park, deserted and gleaming, Berlusconi pointed out that the place and the evening were very romantic, waited for the translators to finish, and then his face split into a sly smile—a very sly smile—and he concluded with the admonishment: "Look out, or tonight we'll be increasing the population."

The next day, he also said that he had never seen such a lovely fountain in all his life.

THIS WAS THE PLACE where everything began, for me. I'm not trying to say that I considered it to be mine and mine alone—quite the opposite, in fact, that had been the moment when I first realized that there were other people. But to go from there to the sight of the most powerful men on Earth at the exact same spot where we had been, me, Massimo, and the freckle-faced kid; to go from there to the sight of Berlusconi, standing in that exact spot—in my spot—and to hear him utter a lascivious and awkward phrase—especially the fact that he was speaking to older people, in all likelihood too old now ever to have children again—with the intention of sharing an ill-restrained excitement; in other words, to see that specific spot in my Palace occupied by the most powerful men on earth, in the same special conditions (closed to the public, enjoyed by only a few) in which I had become part of the world, and at the same time to hear such an unseemly phrase, dripping with a demented, ruinous libido, tantamount to a broad and knowing wink of the eye, sinking to the level of jokes out

Translated by Antony Shugaar • Italian | Italy

of weekly puzzle magazines—gave me an exact perception of the time that had passed; it gave me an exact perception of what had transpired with Berlusconi's election.

And once again, this time, I had the intuition, partial and fleeting, that the purity to which I was so committed—and what time and what place could be any purer than that evening and that fountain?—was too difficult to attain. At least for me. Especially because people were now coming all the way to my home, to rape and ravage it. Especially because I had left and gone away, leaving the field open to them.

In some sense, while on that long-ago early-summer day I had become not only the boy from Caserta who was ransacking a refrigerator, but also one more Italian, at the very moment that I was gaining the awareness of being one; now came the narrative conclusion of that flash of awareness: so many years later, I felt the guilt of having abandoned my city, having left my post guarding that specific and revelatory space in front of the fountain of Diana and Acteon; and as soon as I left, that space had been occupied by the one Italian chosen as the representative of all Italians, in the eyes of the world, and there he was, telling the leaders of the most important nations: What a sparkling evening this is, look out, there's going to be some fucking tonight.

And in fact, the matter of fucking would prove to be, in the years that followed, a not insubstantial part of the private and public life—of the muddled confusion between private and public—of this extremely wealthy businessman who had become Prime Minister.

ON THAT OCCASION, Berlusconi is present in the most public and official version imaginable: he is the Prime Minister of Italy, welcoming the most powerful nations on earth as his guests. And he immediately veers sharply into the realm of the private, the intimacy of the bedroom—a place that would later, in fact, leave its mark on his public life, or should I say his private life in public. He speaks of intimate matters in the presence of the most powerful people on the planet. While I, in the same spot, a great many years earlier, alone, in the most private act possible, in the solitude of a clueless little boy, intuit that there exists a life outside of my own.

Therefore, as far as he and I are concerned, Berlusconi is Acteon who is watching me, and I'm Diana. It doesn't matter that that image condenses together two different points in time, because the scene depicted by the fountain also synthesizes the story, aligning together two different times. The matter between me and Berlusconi, suddenly, on a summer day, had become a personal matter. From that evening on, it would become my job to understand how to deal with it.

Translated by Antony Shugaar • Italian | Italy

Albania's LULJETA LLESHANAKU
grew up under difficult conditions, living
under family house arrest during Enver
Hoxha's communist regime. Her poems are
a response to what was missing then, in her
life and for her whole generation, evoking
absences, emptiness—what was unseen,
unspoken, or undone.

Pothuajse Dje

Ca njerëz të panjohur,
po ngrejnë një shtëpi të re këtu rrotull.
Potère, të shara dhe harè.
Çekiçë dhe derivate krahësh.
Mclodi të fishkëllyera pa fillim dhe fund,
kafshuar nga lemza në të dyja anët.

Dritarja e madhe hapet drejt lindjes.
Një djalë i ngathët me sandale,
tërheq pas vetes një bidon të madh uji sa gjysma e tij,
qetësues, si një letër thithëse mbi bojën e freskët,
para se të kthehet fleta.

Kamionët e ngarkuar me llaç,
lënë simbolin e infinitit
mbi baltë.

Pergjatë murit, një pe- plumbçe ruan drejtimin,
si medalion që varet nga hiçi,
nga qafa e dikujt, të cilit,
askush nuk merr mundimin t'ia shohë fytyrën.
Ata e filluan me hangarin. Kështu fillon çdo jetë e re.
me një aksiomë.

Almost Yesterday

Strangers are building a new house nearby.
They shout, cuss, cheer.
Hammers and a bustle of arms.
They whistle melodies
bookended by hiccups.

The large window opens to the east.
A lazy boy in sandals
drags a large bucket of water half his size.
He's a sedative like blotting paper on fresh ink
before turning the page.

Trucks loaded with cement
leave the symbol of infinity
on dirt.

Along the wall, a plumb line controls direction
like a medallion hanging from nowhere
from someone's neck whose face
nobody bothers to look at.
They started out with the barn. This is how new life begins,
with an axiom.

Befas unë sjell në mend tim atë,
të sapokthyer nga fusha,
gjithë djersë, në pushimin e drekës,
atë dhe time më,
kur dolën nga hangari
duke shtruar me nxitim flokët e ngatërruar,
të skuqur, me shikimin gjithë frikë rrotull
si dy hajdutë.

Dhoma e tyre e gjumit ishte e freskët dhe e pastër
në katin e dytë të shtëpisë.
Unë akoma pyes veten: "Pse në hangar?"
Por, mbaj mend gjithashtu, që gjëja e gjallë dhe të vjelat
nuk ishin të mbara atë vit
dhe se kursenim, dritat fikeshin herët.

Isha dymbëdhjetë vjeç.
Gjumin e kisha të thellë dhe kureshtjen të mefshët,
hedhur pa kujdes
si togjet e dëborës në njërën anë të rrugës.

Por hangarin e mbaj mend qartë, sikur ka ndodhur dje,
pothuajse dje.
Nuk harrohen lehtë gjërat që i sheh duke mbyllur njërin sy,
fundi i heroit në kinema,
apo eklipsi i parë të diellit.

Suddenly, I recall my father
having just returned from the field
all sweaty, during lunch break,
he and mother
coming out of the barn
tidying their tangled hair, in a hurry,
flushed, looking around in fear
like two thieves.

Their bedroom was cool and clean
on the second floor of the house.
I still ask myself: "Why in the barn?"
But I also remember that livestock and harvest
were short that year,
we were on a budget
and switched the lights off early.

I was twelve.
My sleep was deep, my curiosity numb,
thrown carelessly around
like mounds of snow on the side of the road.

But I remember the barn clearly, as if it were yesterday,
almost yesterday.
You cannot easily forget things you watch with one eye closed,
the death of the hero at the movies,
or your first eclipse of the sun.

Qytetet

Ata, qytetet,
janë pak a shumë të njejtë:
drita, plehëra, xhamat e thyer në katin e dytë të shkollës së muzikës
shitës ambulantë dhe banka me shkallare prej mermeri të kuq,
stacione, aromë buke e sapopjekur që i bën të gjithë të barabartë,
ura, gra që plaken nga sytë dhe meshkuj që thinjen nga zëri,
reklama, mëri që kalben në arka zarzavatesh në rrugë,
shira, tjegulla që nxihen dhe varreza që zbardhen,
banda e bashkisë që luan prej tridhjetë vjetësh "Marshin e tartarëve,"
kulla e sahatit me kokën midis reve si dervish në trans, pije freskuese,
dhe një ambulancë e parkuar midis dy botëve.

Nga qendra, gradualisht shtëpia ime dhe e gjithkujt
zhvendoset në periferi,
tek gjymtyrët, duart,
të cilave, nuk u duhet gjuha
për të treguar vendin ku kruhet apo dhemb.

Secilit prej qyteteve të mësoi diçka:
i pari të mësoi vdekjen në një stacion treni, ditën për diell;
i dyti, të jetuarin;
kurse i treti,
çlodhjen agnostike midis të dyve.
Njërin e pushtove natën, në errësirë;
gjarpërinjtë e zbutur në ballin e farmacive
të treguan rrugën. Tjetrin, herët, sa pa mbërthyer akoma kopsat.
Një theks i ri fytyrën ta ndau në dy pjesë,
si vija e flokëve.

Cities

Cities are more or less the same:

lights, garbage, broken windows on the second floor of the music school,

street vendors and banks with red marble staircases,

bus stops, the smell of freshly baked bread equalizing all,

bridges, women who age in the eyes and men who wither in their voices,

billboards, grudges that rot in vegetable cases on street markets,

rains staining roof tiles and bleaching graves,

a municipal band that's been playing "The March of the Tartars" for thirty
      years,

the clocktower with its head in the clouds like a dervish in a trance, fresh
      lemonade,

and an ambulance parked between two worlds.

From the center, gradually, my house and everyone else's

shifts to the periphery,

toward the city's limbs, its hands

which don't need language

to point out where it hurts or itches.

Each city taught you something:

the first about death at a train station—in broad daylight;

the second—how to live;

and the third,

the agnostic respite between the two.

You conquered the first one at night, in the dark;

the tame snakes on pharmacy walls

showed you the way. The other, much earlier, without buttoning yourself.

A new accent split your face in two

like the line that parts the hair.

Translated by Ani Gjika • Albanian | Albania

Secili prej tyre të la një shenjë:
i pari një të çjerrë në vetull, i dyti shtoi disa tjegulla mbi shpatulla,
dhe i treti, disa gropa arsyetimi në sintaksë.

Por, jo ti tek ata...
Qytetet nuk të njohin deri në momentin që ikën, i braktis,
duke lënë pas një këpucë teke në nxitim e sipër,
pas një magjie të mbetur në mes.

Each city left you with a scar:

The first—a scratch on your eyebrow, the second hardened your
    shoulders,

and the third, some logical holes to your syntax.

But you left no mark on them.

Cities don't recognize you until the moment you flee,

escape in a hurry,

leaving behind a single shoe

after a magic trick abandoned halfway through.

Translated by Ani Gjika • Albanian | Albania

Po Afrohet...

Po afrohet. Ndjehet, pa e parë,
siç ndjen praninë e detit që ndodhet diku afër.
Detit ku derdhen gjithë lumenjtë e botës, edhe i yti bashkë me ta,
që nga i ëmbël,
brenda pak sekondave bëhet i kripur,
dhe i hidhur zeher pak më thellë.

Pasqyra zgjohet çdo ditë me humor të keq.
Përtej dritares,
një fushë e pafund zbardh nga lakrat dhe bryma.

Janë vjeljet e vona, dhe asgjë më shumë.
Alarmohesh:
a ke ushqim mjaftueshëm për të kaluar dimrin?

A ke çfarë të përtypësh, a ke çfarë të kujtosh?
Edhe pse disa prej tyre,
akoma kërkojne stomak të fortë.

Pyet të t'ëmë, çfarë di për plakjen. Pyet gratë e moshuara të fisit,
ashtu, të stivosura bukur,
si një takëm lugësh prej argjendi në një kuti kartoni,
në pritje të një darke që mbase nuk vjen kurrë...

Pyeti, si ia dolën? Mbase kanë ndonjë këshillë.
Dhe drejt teje zgjatet po ajo pëllëmbë e ngrohtë dhe e squllët mashtruese
që kur ishe e vogël, të çoi për të shpuar veshët për vathë:
"Nuk të dhemb fare! Është veç një pickim."

Aging

It approaches. I can feel it, without seeing it,
like one feels the presence of nearby waves.
The sea, where all the world's rivers spill, even your own,
even the sweet waters
that in a few seconds turn salty,
and bitter as hell at the deep end.

The mirror wakes up every day in a bad mood.
Beyond the window,
glistens an endless field of frost on cabbages.

It's the late harvest and nothing more.
You're alarmed:
do you have enough food to survive the winter?

Enough to chew on, enough memories?
Although you'll need a strong stomach
for some of them.

Ask your mother what she knows of aging.
Ask the elderly women of your family,
who are lined up beautifully
like silver cutlery in a cardboard box
waiting for a dinner that may never happen...

Ask them, how did they manage it? Perhaps they'll give you advice.
Or they will extend their hand to you
that same warm, clammy, deceiving reach
which, as a kid, once took you to pierce your ears:
"It doesn't hurt a bit. Just a little pinch."

Translated by Ani Gjika • Albanian | Albania

Nuk kanë se ç'të japin. Mësimet janë kaq personale,
si shamia e hundëve, si brisku i rrojes, si një një palë proteza.
Dhe as që e dinë,
që të moshuarit dikur kishin perëndinë e tyre, Saturnin,
që kujdesej për ta, në kohën që i mbetej
nga të vjelat, meditimi për kohën dhe gostitë.

Po afrohet... Do të vazhdojë gjatë dhe pa ngut,
si muzika simfonike që mbush kanalet e radios orëve të vona,
e ndërprerë rrallë për ndonjë lajm të shpejtë,
dhe pa kërkuar ndjesë,
dhe për të vazhduar prapë aje ku e la, në *Toccata et fugue*,
solo me flaut.

They've nothing to give. Aging is so personal,
like the handkerchief, the razor, a pair of dentures.
And they don't even know
that the elderly once had their own god, Saturn,
who looked after them, in the free time
after harvest, a meditation on time and feasts.

It approaches... It will go on for a long while, leisurely,
like a symphony that fills radio channels in late night hours,
interrupted rarely by brief news,
nonapologetic,
then continuing again where it left off, at *Toccata et fugue*,
played by a solo flute.

Translated by Ani Gjika • Albanian | Albania

PATRICIO PRON (born in Rosario, Argentina, in 1975) resided in Germany for nearly a decade. His 2010 collection in which these stories appear offers fascinating portraits of contemporary German life, evidence that, as Faulkner famously wrote, "The past is never dead. It's not even past."

La historia del cazador y del oso #1

Una de las cosas que más le gustaban era contar su vida como si fuera la de otra; y en cierta forma lo era porque todo lo que había vivido se había esfumado. Le había tomado menos tiempo olvidarse de su vida que vivirla, lo cual quizá la hubiera hecho sonreír si hubiese sido consciente de ello; pero no lo era, o no siempre; la mayor parte del tiempo estaba allí sentada en un presente interminable, en el que la falta de referencias anteriores convertía cualquier cosa en una calamidad: la caída de una cuchara al suelo mientras comía, la lluvia en el rostro una mañana que había amanecido despejada o la visita de alguien que decía conocerla. Pero no había muchas personas que la visitaran: su hija ella decía que era su hija y un muchacho ruso, casi un adolescente, que a veces le hacía hacer movimientos con los brazos o le mostraba fotografías o, la mayor parte de las veces, se sentaba y la miraba y le contaba sus problemas. Ella suponía que se los contaba porque sabía que no iba a recordarlos luego. No tenía importancia; ella escuchaba y en ocasiones opinaba una cosa u otra, de acuerdo al tenor de las confesiones del muchacho ruso. Muchas veces éste le contaba de sus dificultades con el dinero o le hablaba de sus compañeros de piso, otros dos rusos que bebían demasiado y solían pelear continuamente con los vecinos y entre sí, o del clima o de lo que había aprendido esa mañana en el curso de enfermería al que asistía desde que había llegado de Rusia, un año atrás. No es que las historias fueran muy interesantes, pero el muchacho ruso sabía contarlas, . . .

Translated by
KATHLEEN HEIL

The Story of the Hunter and the Bear #1

One of the things she liked most was to tell her story as though it belonged to someone else; and in a way it did, because everything she'd lived had evaporated. It took her less time to forget about her life than to live it, which might have made her smile had she been conscious of this; but she wasn't, or not always; most of the time she was situated in an interminable present, in which the lack of prior references rendered any incident a calamity: a cockroach landing on the floor while she was eating, the rain on her face on a morning that began with clear skies, or a visit from someone who claimed to know her. Not that many people visited: her daughter—she claimed she was her daughter—and a Russian boy, a teenager, practically, who would sometimes make her move her arms or show her photographs, or, more often, would sit and stare at her and tell her his problems. She figured he told them to her because he knew that later she wouldn't remember. It didn't matter; she listened, and would sometimes offer advice, when the nature of the Russian boy's confessions called for it. Often, he'd recount his money troubles or tell her about his roommates, two other Russians who drank too much and fought more or less continuously with the neighbors and among themselves, or he'd talk about the weather or what he had learned that morning in the nursing classes he'd been attending since coming from Russia the year before. It's not that these stories were terribly interesting, but the Russian boy knew how to tell them, making up for his

Translated by Kathleen Heil • Spanish | Argentina

limited vocabulary with gestures or words in Russian that she didn't understand but that, in any case, she could comprehend in the contexts in which
he'd say them. Sometimes, when the boy had already left, she believed she
remembered what he'd recounted, snippets of conversation or—even better—whole sentences that she remembered he'd said, such as, "My second
exam is tomorrow, but I'm not prepared," or "I have a crush on this girl in
my class named Eva who's tall and has brown eyes," but she was never
certain whether these were things the Russian boy had told her or if she'd
imagined them. Maybe he'd only mentioned a classmate named Eva and
she'd inferred from the way he said her name that he liked her, and then,
maybe, thinking about an Eva that she knew, she'd imagined that the Russian's Eva was tall and had brown eyes. Sometimes, she'd make a mental
note to ask the Russian boy about Eva, but then forget. Often, if she was
looking out the window or doing anything else, anything that took her attention *outside* of herself, she'd come back to herself and to consideration of
her condition, completely forgetting what that condition was; and for a
second she'd feel once again like the person she'd been when she could still
remember things, and she'd wonder whether the entirety of her condition
wasn't actually feigned, or the product of distraction, rather than an irreversible disease. Her daughter, the woman who came three times a day to
feed and dress her, who claimed she was her daughter, would respond that
she was mistaken when she would say she didn't believe there was anything
wrong with her; then, out of spite, she would recite some lines from Heine
or Schiller or Goethe to show her that her head wasn't completely empty
just yet, but her daughter would respond that those were the last drops and
that they'd also dry up; in any case, there was something strange about the
fact that she could remember whole stanzas learned as a teenager, primarily
from her father. She had a very large library, a library made up of dozens of
first editions that her father had looked after and treasured, which must be
worth a lot of money and which her daughter would sometimes stare at for
a long time, as though wondering what to do with them; each time she'd
catch her daughter doing this, she'd tell her that these books were family
heirlooms and would never be sold, and her daughter would dismiss the
statement with a wave of her hand and then turn to vacuuming or doing
anything else to keep herself busy and distant in the minutes spent in her
home. Still, an image seemed to stick in her head, like a leaf refusing to slip

through a storm drain on a rainy day: her father putting these books into boxes and storing the boxes in the cellar, locking it and putting the key in his inner coat pocket, and then grabbing a suitcase and leaving the house as the sound of bombs—which, in any case, she would have been used to by then—loomed ever closer and more threatening. Her mother cried upon leaving, but her father just looked straight ahead, in search of a truck or car that would take them into town, where there was no combat. Was there anything worse for someone like her father than to have to leave his books behind, this thread uniting his family and a culture, two things this war seemed to want to reduce to rubble? she'd sometimes think, even though she also wasn't sure she hadn't made this up, too, or taken it from a book she'd read. Maybe she'd read about a similar event in some book about Napoleon's invasion of Germany, maybe her father had never left his books behind and had been able to accommodate these new circumstances the way he'd been able to accommodate the previous ones and the previous ones, or had effectively abandoned his home but taken the books with him. In the end, the books were there, and one afternoon she found the Russian boy staring at them, too. That afternoon, the Russian boy told her a Russian story that his Russian father would often tell him when he was a little Russian boy. It was the story of a hunter who needed a pelt to protect himself from the approaching winter and went out in search of a bear, but the bears were already hibernating—even though the Russian boy didn't use the word "hibernate" but something similar, she still understood what he meant—or the bears were elsewhere, and the hunter couldn't find a single one. An enormous bear, the only one awake and too clever, perhaps, to be a bear, preferred, instead of hibernating, to spend its winters watching water rush beneath the frozen streams or to shake the trees, letting the snow collected on the branches fall and cover it, but the bear had a problem: it was hungry, and there wasn't much to eat in the forest in winter. One day—this was inevitable—the hunter and the bear finally met. The hunter brought his gun to his shoulder to shoot but couldn't because the trigger was frozen owing to the harsh winter, and the bear, which was too clever to be a bear, realized this and threw itself on the man, swallowing him whole. And so, the Russian boy said, though it might seem that the story ended cruelly, it didn't, he said, since, as happens in all Russian stories, the bear got what it wanted, which was food, and the hunter got what he needed, which was warmth. This was

ÓNLIBÚCAÉ

35

Translated by Kathleen Heil • Spanish | Argentina

the story the Russian boy told, while outside the sun hid behind buildings. One or maybe two days later—it was all the same to her—the Russian boy asked her if she remembered the story of the hunter and the bear, but she didn't know how to respond. That day the Russian boy told her that he needed money urgently because he hadn't passed his exam and as a result he'd have to study an extra semester. She nodded quietly; she genuinely liked the Russian boy: his sincerity and his way of speaking, gesturing and filling in the gaps with Russian words. Sometimes, the Russian boy would show her photos and ask her to tell him what they reminded her of. So she'd make something up; she never accepted that she didn't actually remember the circumstances under which they were taken or whom they portrayed. A blonde woman who might have been her appeared in several, but other people appeared in others, and there were even pictures that looked like they were taken from a magazine. She'd make up stories for all of them: if the picture was of a blonde woman leaning against a car in the sun, she'd say that it was a photo of her in Berlin's Tiergarten in 1954; if another was of a man with his arms around a child, she'd say it was a picture of her husband and daughter that had been taken on her daughter's first day of school. Often, if she was in a good mood and wanted to entertain the Russian boy, she'd tell him everything that'd happened on that day, the

She wanted to say something to him about it, but for some reason couldn't; she remained there, seated, trembling in the darkness...

way she'd dressed her daughter and how she'd accompanied her to school and the way her daughter trembled when she left her at the entrance. The Russian boy always took notes on the back of the photos, and, one day when he went to the bathroom for a moment, she had a chance to read them: on the back of the photo of the man with the girl, the Russian boy had written: "02/26 A brother of hers who died in the war and his daughter," "02/28 Her father with her," "02/03 A TV presenter and a girl who won a contest," "03/04 Her husband with their daughter on the daughter's first day of school," "03/06 A friend of hers named Hans and his daughter on the day they both died in a car accident," and so on. The Russian boy came back from the bathroom and, holding up a photo, asked her who was in it. She said it was a picture of a TV presenter and a girl who'd won a contest, and then she told him what the contest was about, which questions the girl had gotten right and which she'd gotten wrong. The Russian boy smiled and never showed her that photo again. One day—perhaps weeks or months had gone by since he'd told her the story of the hunter and the bear, or merely days—she saw him take a book from the bookshelf and tuck it beneath his sweater before leaving. She wanted to say something to him about it, but for some reason couldn't; she remained there, seated, trembling in the darkness while her hurt and indignation over the theft transformed into a hurt and indignation that was baseless, something that passed through her and pained her although she was unable to articulate why, as when a child is bitten by a dog she'd wanted to pet and for a moment everything she thought she knew and held correct falls apart. Sometime later, the following day, perhaps, she forgot all about it; before showing her the photographs, the Russian boy told her that he'd paid for his course and would be able to continue studying. His voice held something like gratitude in it, but she wasn't able to articulate why. So then he showed her one of the photos, one taken of her with the girl sometime after she'd come back from the hospital, while they were strolling through a park exhausted by winter with bare trees that looked like a giant's hands coming up from the ground in search of more life and more worry and more hope, and she told the Russian boy it was a picture of one of her husband's sisters named Sabine who had a daughter and the daughter was now a schoolteacher in Regensburg, and the Russian boy wrote a few things down and then got up to turn on a lamp.

Translated by Kathleen Heil • Spanish | Argentina

La historia del cazador y del oso #4

Una mujer con el cabello rubio y corto le dice que lo que a ella más le gust-aba cuando estaba bien era contar su vida como si fuera la de otro. La mujer lleva el cabello a la altura de los hombros y sus puntas están erizadas por la electricidad. Quizá no sea muy vieja, aunque lo parece. "¿Quién eres?" le pregunta ella. "Soy tu hija," dice la otra. Ella anota todo con un lápiz antes de que se le olvide.

La mujer del cabello corto tiene una llave y entra a la casa cuando el sol sube y cuando el sol se pone y la viste y le da de comer. Si pasa algo que no ha planeado, si la mujer tira la cuchara al piso o si el día se arruina y llueve, se enoja, y la otra no sabe qué hacer. Un día, hoy, después de darle de comer, la mujer del cabello corto pone la televisión y lava un plato o pasa la aspira-dora. Nunca le pregunta a la mujer cómo está. "Si eres mi hija," le dice un día, "eres una mala hija." "No importa lo que pienses de mí," le responde la hija, "mañana no te acordarás de lo que has dicho, pero yo sí. Y un día me marcharé y te vas a joder, ya lo verás," le dice la hija.

No alcanza con anotarlo todo. También hay que saber dónde encajar cada nota. Y no se puede anotarlo todo, sólo algunas cosas, porque si las notas son muy largas ella se olvida por la mitad de por qué las toma.

La mujer del cabello corto termina de pasar la aspiradora y mira el reloj y luego camina hasta las estanterías y se queda mirándolas. Ella sabe un poco más de eso. Sabe que son los libros de su padre, todas primeras ediciones de libros clásicos de la literatura alemana que su padre reunió durante años. . . .

The Story of the Hunter and the Bear #4

A woman with short blonde hair tells her that what she most enjoyed doing when she was doing well was to talk about her life as though it belonged to someone else. The woman has shoulder-length hair with frayed, staticky ends. She might not be very old, even though she looks it. "Who are you?" she asks her. "I'm your daughter," the other one answers. She writes everything down with a pencil before she forgets.

The woman with short hair has a key and enters the house when the sun rises and when it sets, dressing and feeding her. If something unanticipated happens, if the woman throws the spoon to the floor or if the day is ruined by rain, she gets upset, and the other one doesn't know what to do. One day, today, after feeding her, the woman with short hair turns the TV on and washes dishes or vacuums. She never asks the woman how she's doing. "If you're my daughter," she says to her one day, "you're a bad daughter." "It doesn't matter what you think of me," the daughter responds, "by tomorrow you won't remember what you've said, but I will. And one day I'm going to walk out of here and you'll be screwed, you'll see," the daughter tells her.

She isn't able to write everything down. And she also has to know where to hide each note. It's not possible to write it all down, just a few things, because if the notes are too long she forgets halfway through why she's writing them.

The woman with short hair finishes vacuuming and glances at her watch and then walks to the shelves and stands there staring at them. She knows a

Translated by Kathleen Heil • Spanish | Argentina

little more. She knows that these books belonged to her father, that they're all first editions, classics of German literature that her father collected over the years. She knows they're worth their weight in gold, but also knows that they're something like a record of her father and that, if she makes an effort, they'll allow her to recall a story. "Maybe we should get rid of one or two," the daughter says. "We're never going to sell them," the other one says. "You're a miserable old woman," the daughter says. "You disgust me. And now you can forget what I've just told you," she says.

Later, today, the doorbell rings and the woman with short hair answers. A young man comes in. She walks toward them and she tells her: "It's Yuri, talk to him." And Yuri says: "I'm Yuri, do you remember me?" And she says: "Of course."

Yuri makes her raise and lower her arms. Her legs, too. She doesn't remember this when she's taking her notes, but she can still feel the pain in her limbs, which is why she knows she's raised and lowered her arms and also her legs, too. Then he shows her some photos. "Who's this?" he asks. A blonde woman has her arms around a girl. "That's me," she says. "Who's this?" he asks, showing her another photo. "That's me," she says, but the picture looks like it was taken from a magazine. "That's not me," she says. "Who's this?" he asks. "That's me," she says.

She furtively takes notes when the Russian boy goes to the bathroom or when he stares at the bookshelves with his back to her, as though he'd forgotten what he'd been doing moments before.

If she'd been capable of remembering things, if she weren't incapacitated, she would have remembered that Yuri is studying to be a nurse, that he had come to this country one year earlier, that he lives with two other Russians who drink too much, and that he often sits and tells her about his problems, perhaps because he thinks she'll forget them immediately, that she'll listen and offer advice when needed, based on what the Russian boy, who always has money troubles, tells her. It's not that what he recounts is terribly interesting, but the Russian boy is good at telling stories, he gestures and says things in Russian when he can't remember how to say them in German. She doesn't understand these Russian words but can imagine their meaning based on the intonation the Russian boy uses and the context in which he uses them. Most of all she can understand how the Russian boy feels because the same thing happens to her. The Russian boy fills in the gaps of what he can't recall with words in German, and she fills the gaps of what she can't recall with notes.

And when the sun goes down the Russian boy leaves and a while later the woman with short hair arrives. The woman with short hair is carrying an enormous bag of bread. "Where'd you get that bread?" she asks her. "I work in a bakery," she says to the other one and turns on the TV.

"I can't believe you're wasting your time on that," the woman with short hair says to the other one when she sees her taking notes. "Don't you realize that, even if you take thousands of notes, you're never going to be able to remember what they're about? You won't even remember that you've taken them," she tells her.

Nevertheless, it's possible her condition is less serious than the others believe it to be since, if she makes an effort, she can remember what they've told her, snippets of conversation, stray sentences from the Russian boy, such as: "My second exam is tomorrow, but I'm not prepared," or "I have a crush on this girl in my class named Eva, who's tall and has brown eyes." The woman with short hair sits beside her in a chair facing the TV and brings a spoon to her lips. So she tells her: "He has a crush on this girl in his class named Eva who's tall and has brown eyes." "Quit talking nonsense," the other one says.

Maybe she imagined it, in whole or in part. Maybe he told her he had a crush on a classmate but never said her name. Maybe he simply mentioned a classmate named Eva and she'd inferred from the way he said her name that he liked her. Maybe later she thought of an Eva she once knew and imagined that the Russian's Eva was like her, tall and with brown eyes. Maybe she really doesn't remember anything. Maybe it's true that her brain has erased her entire life in less time than it's taken her to live it and now it's just a matter of filling in those gaps, but, then, why does she remember this Eva?

The woman with short hair undresses her and tucks her in bed, and then tries to take from her the pages where she writes down her notes. She resists, and the other one scoffs and leaves her alone. She lies down beside her and turns off the light. "Do you happen to know an Eva?" she asks her, but the woman with short hair has already fallen asleep or doesn't feel like answering.

If she wakes up before her daughter does, if her attention is momentarily taken outside of herself, she comes back to herself without taking notice of

Translated by Kathleen Heil • Spanish | Argentina

her condition and thinks she's the same person she must have been when she could still remember things, and then she wonders whether the entirety of her condition isn't feigned, or the product of a series of distractions, rather than an irreversible disease. If her daughter happens to be the one to wake her, the day is already ruined.

While waiting for the woman with short hair to return and feed her, she wonders why, if her condition is irreversible, she's able to remember entire stanzas of poems that come from the books on her bookshelves, she thinks, or why she has clear memories of her father putting these books in boxes and storing those boxes in the cellar and locking the cellar door with a key and placing the key in the inside pocket of his coat, a brown coat, and then grabbing a suitcase and leaving the house with her while around them the sound of explosions, which is a sound she's gotten used to, moves closer and closer. And of her mother.

She reads over her previous notes while sitting by the window and then writes some more. Her mother cries when they leave their home behind and, as she walks, turns to look back, but her father looks straight ahead, searching for a car or truck that can take them to his parents' village where there's no longer any combat. Is there anything worse for someone like her father than to have to leave his books behind, this thread uniting his family and a culture, the two things this war was reducing to rubble? she thinks. And then the memory grows faint somehow, and she thinks that maybe she's made this up as well or taken it from one of the books she's read. Perhaps her father never left his books behind and was able to accommodate these new circumstances the way he'd been able to accommodate the previous ones and the previous ones, or had effectively abandoned his home but taken the books with him. In the end, the books are there, and in and around them are stories that she remembers.

> *She's sitting in the darkness, waiting, but doesn't know what for.*

The woman with the short hair comes back at noon and finds her going over her notes and smiles ironically, and then she recounts the story of her father and the books and asks her why, if she's sick, she can remember this story, and the other one says: "It's the last thing you've got left. You'll wind up forgetting this, too, you're going to die with an empty head." So then she recites, trembling, shouting nearly, a passage from one of the books, but the other one says nothing, and she's so agitated that afterward she can barely write down what happened.

Later, today, the doorbell rings and the woman with short hair answers. And a young man comes in. She walks toward them and she tells her: "It's Yuri, talk to him." And Yuri says: "I'm Yuri, do you remember me?" And she says: "Of course."

Yuri shows her some photos. "Who's this?" he asks her. In the picture a blonde woman has her arms around a little girl. "A TV presenter," she says. "Who's this?" he asks her, showing her another. "That's my sister," she says, but the picture looks like it was taken from a magazine. "No, it's the TV presenter," she says. "Who's this?" he asks her, showing her another photo of a blonde woman with her arms around a little girl. "That's my sister," she says.

That afternoon the Russian boy tells her a Russian story. It's the story of a hunter who needs a pelt in order to protect himself from the approaching winter, which is very harsh, and he heads out in search of a bear, but the bears are already hibernating, though this isn't the word Yuri uses, but rather one in Russian that she nonetheless understands, and only one is awake, a very clever bear that's also very hungry, and the hunter and the bear finally meet and the hunter can't shoot because the trigger on his rifle is frozen owing to the harsh winter and the bear swallows him whole, and so, Yuri says, as happens in all Russian stories, the bear gets what it wants, which is food, and the hunter what he needs, which is warmth. And afterward Yuri is silent for some time and then he stares for a moment longer at the bookshelves and leaves.

Sometime later, perhaps one or two days later or maybe that same day, the door opens and a young man walks in, who says: "I'm Yuri, do you remember me?" And she says: "Of course." Then Yuri bends her arms and legs until they're very sore and then he sits and asks her if she remembers the story he told her, the story of the hunter and the bear, but she doesn't remember anything and she says no, she doesn't remember anything, and then he gets up and takes one of the books from the shelves and tucks it beneath his sweater and leaves, and she tries to shout but can't, and she remains there, alone in the house, trembling with indignation, not knowing what to do.

She's sitting in the darkness, waiting, but doesn't know what for. She feels unsettled, but doesn't know why. She wonders if she'll be able to read the notes she's taken once someone turns on a light or if things will happen as they did once before, when she stayed up all night taking notes only to discover the next morning that they were illegible. There are sounds at the door and a woman with short blonde hair comes in. "Who are you?" she asks her. "I'm your daughter," the other woman says. She writes everything down with a pencil before she forgets.

Later, today, the doorbell rings and the woman with short hair answers. A young man comes in. She walks toward them and she tells her: "It's Yuri, talk to him." And Yuri says: "I'm Yuri, do you remember me?" And she says: "Of course."

Yuri asks her if she remembers a story he told her about a hunter and a bear, but she doesn't remember anything and she says no, she doesn't remember anything, and then he says his exam didn't go well and he's going to have to study an extra semester and he's already paid for it and she senses gratitude and shame in his voice without knowing why but nods quietly. Then Yuri shows her some photos. "Who's this?" he asks her. The picture is of a blonde woman with her arms around a little girl. "That's a sister of mine named Eva," she says. "Who's this?" he asks her, showing her another photo. "That's me," she says, but the picture looks like it was taken from a magazine. "One moment," Yuri says and gets up to go to the bathroom, and she takes advantage of this opportunity to look at the pictures he's left on the table: a woman who could be her appears in several, but other people appear in others, and there are even pictures that look as though they were taken from a magazine. On the back of one in which the blonde woman appears with a little girl strolling through a park with bare trees that look like a giant's hands coming up from the ground in search of more life and more worry and more hope, someone has written: "02/26 A sister of hers named Heidi strolling with her daughter in a park in Gelsenkirchen," "02/28 Her mother with her," "03/02 A TV presenter and a girl who won a contest," "03/04 Her with her daughter on the first day of school," "03/06 A friend of hers named Sabine and her daughter the day they both died in a car accident." Then the Russian boy comes back from the bathroom and she puts the photos back on the table and the boy picks up one in which a blonde woman is strolling with a little girl through a park with bare trees that look like a giant's hands coming up from the ground in search of more life and more worry and more hope. "Who's this," he asks, and she thinks she should tell the truth, but she also thinks that maybe she's paying for something terrible she did in the past, something she doesn't remember, and says: "That's one of my brother's sisters who lived in Regensburg during the war," and then the boy smiles and gets up to turn on a lamp.

Translated by Kathleen Heil • Spanish | Argentina

LUZ PICHEL was born in the Galician province of Pontevedra in 1947. In these poems, Pichel's haptic experience of her home village fractures and multiplies inside what she calls a "forest of memory"; the poems that emerge portray not only a place but also a way of being in the world.

Poema prólogo

Hai nesta aldea un gato
que coñece os abismos.

Ás noites,
desde o Alto das Penas
érguese e mira para a casa que fora do seu dono
e laia coma un cadelo adoecido.
A súa sombra é longa e afiada.
Espétaselle a un no peito de por vida.

Vai haber que o matar.

Prologue

In this village there's a cat
who knows the abyss.

At night,
from atop Alto das Penas
he stands and looks down at the house that was his master's
and howls like a wounded puppy.
His shadow is long and sharp.
It sinks into your chest, lodges there for good.

We will have to kill him.

É mediodía

Miro polo postigo da porta dos monicreques.
A calor do verán faise pesada ás dúas da tarde
cando as follas da cerdeira non tremen
nin se escoita ladrar.
Á sombra tranquila da cerdeira
entre os gatos e os cans
e a la das ovellas que unha muller espile,
unha rolada de nenos medio nus
folga e dorme,
mamando no dedo gordo da man ou do pé
cos xeonllos pegados ao peito
e o lombo arqueado.

A la espelida fai montón moi grande,
vaise estendendo por riba dos nenos
que dormen nunha nube.

Nin medo nin frío
uns achegados aos outros
no seo brando da herba
que medrou coa chuvia.

Mesturados cos nenos
unha camada de gatiños de días
mama da súa nai, que tira a cabeza atrás
para facerlles sitio.

A muller que espile a la das ovellas
parece que fala soa.
Arrimadà ao tronco da cerdeira
cotea co sono.

Midafternoon

I look through in the hole in the puppet door.
The summer heat presses down at two in the afternoon
when the leaves of the cherry tree don't rustle
and the barking goes silent.
In the shade of the cherry tree
among the dogs and cats
and the sheep wool a woman cards,
a litter of half-naked children
rests and dozes
sucking on their thumbs or their big toes
knees to their chests
backs rounded.

The carded wool forms a huge pile,
begins to spread out over the children
who sleep in a cloud.

No cold or fear
each one close to the others
in the soft bosom of grass
brought up by the rain.

Mixed in among the children
a litter of newborn kittens
nurses on their mother, who throws her head back
to make room for them.

The woman carding wool
seems to be talking to herself.
Leaning into the cherry tree
grazing sleep.

Translated by Neil Anderson • Galician | Spain

Unha cereixa podre caeu da árbore na cara dun neno e espertouno.

Métea na boca o neno sen saber o que traga.

Sigue durmindo,

aproveitando o tempo.

O can da casa,

que miraba por todos sen cerrar ollo,

érguese e vaise cara á burata fondísima da Chousa Vella:

compre mirar tamén polo gando morto.

A rotten cherry falls from the tree onto a child's face and wakes him.
He puts it in his mouth and swallows absently.
He keeps sleeping,
lulled by the heat.

The farm dog,
who's been watching over them all,
gets up and heads for the great pit near Chousa Vella:
it's time now to look in on the dead livestock.

ÓNL私IBÚCAÉ

Translated by Neil Anderson • Galician | Spain

Coidar
os pementos

Mirei polo burato do postigo da porta
dos monicreques
e vin os dous nenos do fillo de Celso
apañando cagallóns de cabalo
e meténdoos nun cesto
para lle levar aos pementos do porral.
Cerrei os ollos e os nenos dos cagallóns
eramos ti e máis eu,
que fuxiramos a escape do retrato da familia
saltando valados.

Tending the Peppers

I looked through the hole
in the puppet theater door
and saw Celso's grandkids
collecting horseshit
and putting it in a basket
to take over to the pepper starts.
I closed my eyes and the horseshit kids
were you and me,
hopping fences
running off to escape the family portrait.

Translated by Neil Anderson • Galician | Spain

O que se
ve mirando

Mirei polo poxigo da porta dos monicreques
e vin as noces na nogueira
a herba no prado
a tapa do pozo negro ao ras do chan
á beira do pozo negro
un loureiro nacendo entre as pedras do valo
unha malva pequena que escapou da gadaña
e é boa para durmir
un cabalo ao galope polo ceo adiante
camiño de Fisterra.

Adrián, algo sucio e queimado do sol,
mátase a rir mirando brincar a galiña
despois de morta.

Todo está no seu sitio.
Xa me podo marchar.

What You See When You Look

I looked out through the hole in the puppet theater door
and saw the walnuts in their tree
the grass in the field
the black well-cap along the ground
orange calendula
edging the black well
a bay sapling being born from the stone wall
a mallow that the sickle missed
good for sleep
a horse galloping across the sky
on its way to Fisterra.

Adrián, dirty and sunburned,
laughs watching the hen jump
after she's dead.

Everything is in its place.
I can go now.

Translated by Neil Anderson • Galician | Spain

NATSUKO KURODA was awarded the prestigious Akutagawa Prize in 2013. Her original Japanese story indicates no gender in the characters. Here, the translator has chosen the second-person narrative to avoid making gender explicit.

道の声

　なつかしむほどは遠のいていたのでもない静かな道をたどってきたまひるの帰郷者を，十ねんぐらいまえまでたいていの者がそう呼んでいた名がそう呼んだ．呼ばれた者は立ちどまって見まわしたが，それきりで，植えならべて壁状に刈りととのえた常緑広葉樹の若芽に，こまかくせわしく日があそんでいるばかりだ．

　声のぬしは，かつてこの垣うちに住んでいたのだったと，聞くとどうじにわかった者は，だが人づてのしょうそくによればいまは海彼にいるはずともどうじにおもいだして判じまどい，そらみみかとたしかめたいのなら声のぬしの名を，十ねんまえたいていの者がそう呼んでいた名で呼びかえせばいいのにまあいをはずした．

　もともとその垣うちは，そこの一族のあいだでさまざまに使いまわされていて，おも屋とわたりろうかでつながった小ぶりの二かい屋，すこし離れて平屋，番小屋，住めば住める広さの物おき，一どだけ中であそんだことのある中ばしごつきの土蔵とちらばるそれぞれに，教育集団や仕事先や生死縁組みにつれておりふしに住み手がいれかわるのを見知ってきて，声のぬしがまたそれらのどこかに住みもどってきたのかとも，たまさかに泊りにきているのかともいろいろにかんがえられることにみだされてとっさの呼びかえしをしそこねた者は，もういっぺん呼ぶかと，すこしのま枝葉の壁を透かし見ていたあと，ついあいまいに歩きだしてしまっていた．

　立ちどまるという反応はされたのだから，そのままならそのままにし...

Translated by
ANGUS TURVILL

The Voice on the Road

You had been away but not so long as to feel nostalgic as you walked along the quiet road at noontime. You heard a name calling you, the name almost everyone had called you until about ten years before. You stopped and looked around. Silence. Nothing but the restless, minute play of sunlight among the fresh shoots of the broad-leaved evergreen bushes that lined the road, cut in the shape of a wall.

You knew straight away that the voice belonged to a person who used to live beyond the hedge; but at the same time you remembered being told that the person was overseas, so you couldn't feel sure. All you had to do to check whether it was your imagination was call back, call out the name that almost everyone had called that person ten years before. But the moment passed.

You knew that the premises beyond the hedge had accommodated different members of the family at different times. They'd lived there for various periods, according to the demands of education, employment, birth, death, marriage, and so on. There were several buildings available on the grounds besides the main residence—a small two-story annex, a bungalow, a watchman's house, a shed that was large enough to live in, and a white-painted storehouse, with a fixed ladder inside, where you had once played. Perhaps the person whose voice you'd heard had come back to live in one of these, or just happened to be staying for a while. Distracted by the various possibilities, you lost the opportunity to call straight back. You wondered if

Translated by Angus Turvill • Japanese | Japan

the person might call out again, and peered for a while through the wall of leaves and branches, before walking vaguely on.

Had the person seen you stop and decided, in the absence of any further reaction, to leave it at that? Had the call been speculative, and your lack of response been taken as a type of answer in itself? You had no way of knowing. The situation was inconclusive. And so the call became stranded in the air. It seemed to mock, yet pleadingly pursue; it seemed earnest, yet half in jest. But anyway, it was altogether too unexpected, and you felt no alternative but to put it down to imagination. Over the long years that followed you remembered it sometimes, and it troubled you and then one day you had news that the person whose voice it was had died. But this made no difference. Whatever the facts were, the name that had been caught fast in the air above the road when you were both young, when you had both just finished your education, couldn't be brought down. Even if nobody would ever call you it again, the name was left there, together with the other childhood name, the one that in the end you'd been unable to call back.

> *The children's shouts and songs, the playful chants of parting at dusk would float over the road in a long narrow layer of voice.*

There was no shrine or temple in the vicinity, let alone a park, so it was only natural for the children to play in the road, and it was beside this long, thick wall of broad-leaf evergreen that they normally gathered. The road was narrow, as roads were before cars were common, but it was flat and straight, and even if something that had been hit or thrown landed somewhere off the road it could normally be gotten back without apologizing, at least if one of the children lived there. When anybody wanted, they could have water to wash with or drink as well. There were regulars from most of the houses on both sides of the road, right up to where the line of bushes gave out onto fields with clumps of different herbs. And the buildings were set back from the road, so there were hardly ever complaints. If something got caught in a branch it was just a question of clambering up a stone wall and shaking the tree.

It was normally just the elementary school children who played on the road, so faces changed a lot over time, but when you were in it the group was generally up to fifteen- or sixteen-strong. The children's shouts and songs, the playful chants of parting at dusk would float over the road in a long narrow layer of voice. Eventually, the road was tarmacked and the number of cars grew; children inevitably stopped gathering there to play. But even then this layer of riddle-like, spell-like fragments of song continued to float above the road, and that call sent up out of kilter with its time, its very existence uncertain, continued to be abandoned.

THE PIECE OF PAPER on which you were asked to draw the moon was of normal proportions and so you placed it on the table with the short sides horizontal and proceeded to draw a moon about ten days old, in other words somewhat fatter than a semicircle. You drew it on a slight slant with the pencil line reaching almost to the edge of the paper all the way around. You were looked at in astonishment.

Ordinarily, you were told, people treated the paper as the sky and drew a three- or four-day moon toward the top. Alternatively, they drew a round moon, adding particular animals or vegetation to ensure it wouldn't be mistaken for the sun. Yes, you thought, I could have done that. After all, I was told to draw "the moon," not "only the moon." To make it clear it *was* the moon I could have drawn the silhouette of a bird, or some autumnal grasses bending in the wind.

You were of an age when, nothing else having occurred to you, you went straight ahead and followed your impulse. But you were also already of an age when you could quickly change perspective, and see that your "obvious" was not necessarily the same as everyone else's "obvious." The person who gave you the paper, some three years older than you, presumably wasn't testing you or trying to find anything out; it was just a bit of a game in the form of a watered-down psychological test. But you felt a vague fear take root that one of the children you played with, the one of whom you were always very conscious, might draw the moon in the same way, using the whole piece of paper, marking a simple outline right to its edge, so that it was almost as if nothing had been drawn there at all. Or would the person draw a large perfectly round moon that stretched right across the short dimension of the sheet? Or to show that the paper was too small would the person draw lines right up to the edge, leaving the moon open on one side? Or perhaps scorning such reactions and establishing a distance, the person would draw a slender moon sinking a mountain range.

Both of you had to be complete and so for you, who'd been there first and remained a short while longer, these several hundred days were characterized by clouds of discontent—irritation that itself was irritating, resentment that you resented feeling. For the one who came later and moved on first was it just an unremarkable diversion? But then even after those few hundred days the other child didn't go completely. There were several vaguely intervening years, after you'd both dropped out of the group and gone to different schools, when you would see each other occasionally. Your paths would cross by chance in the street sometimes, or at the station. You'd pass each other with formal bows that would have seemed odd for your age. There is nothing strange about neighbors who've played together as young children not being very close when they are older. Perhaps odder than not getting along was being particularly conscious of it. Not even the simplest of greetings was exchanged, no word on the weather. You simply bowed in silence. As if following the pattern established on the morning you'd met long ago, you were both almost comically stiff. But neither had done anything wrong, neither had any obstinate sense of pride. Something that you could have loosened at any time remained unloosened, and the distance grew.

The child was joining a class below you, so the parent came and asked if, for the first week, you'd walk with the child to school. You'd probably been suggested as a suitable friend by their relatives who lived in the main residence, and the parent probably thought it would help the child settle into the area. The parent may never have considered that things might not be so simple, but neither you, somehow allotted the responsibility, nor the newly arrived, hard-shelled nine-year-old could really cope with the situation. Your parents came out to the gate to see you off and you walked away together. You must have asked the other child at least some questions at first, but looking back on it, all you could remember was a journey of complete silence. It's true you weren't necessarily that good with people, but you weren't the type to make other children feel uncomfortable; you weren't gloomy, and if there hadn't been strong signs of rejection from the nine-year-old, for your part you would certainly not have kept silent.

It was a while later that you realized you weren't being rejected as a friend, but as a superior. And in retrospect, on that first morning you hadn't hesitated to treat the nine-year-old as a very ordinary younger child. After several awkward mornings, the parent came to your house to say thank you, that the child was used to things now, and thus you were relieved of your responsibility, but you were never relieved of the adults' feeling that things had not gone well, of the feeling of guilt that this had been your failure as the elder of the two.

The child that had refused to accept inferior status had no difficulty blending into the group on the road, quickly picked everything up, and within no time was at its very center. At school after just one term the child was chosen as class representative. Halfway down the classroom corridor was a notice board where especially good drawings and compositions were displayed. With the big gaps in achievement between different grades at elementary school, the work of the older pupils was readily admired by the younger ones. But in spite of not being in the top year the child frequently had work displayed and so became known throughout the school. One week when you had your own work displayed you began wondering if the younger one had noticed. But you didn't want to wonder. It was mortifying.

Soon after the younger child arrived, before its achievements were very obvious, you overheard words of praise in a conversation between adults. One of the adults was from your own home and so you later asked what they had been saying. In response you were told all sorts of things about the reputation the nine-year-old had for being so clever, gifted in every way. You didn't hide your disappointment that the praise hadn't been for you. The adult tutted. "Did you really think you were so bright?" The person who said this was someone who'd brought you up, someone with whom you felt no awkwardness, to whom you could say something mistaken without any embarrassment. And so for a while it seemed a double shock, a double disappointment. Perhaps the adult's reaction was simply a kind of belated self-reproach for always having flattered you too much, but nevertheless as the days went by you began to flinch and fret deep inside. You realized for the first time that someone who had always boasted of you, whose words of absolute praise you had never had cause to doubt, could give a more sober judgment based on comparison between you and other children.

THE ROAD WAS LONG and narrow and the children came out at different times depending on their age and school, so even if they all started as one

Translated by Angus Turvill • Japanese | Japan

group they'd often split up into two or three, each chanting different songs. Then as evening came and the number fell those who remained might join together again as a single group. Sometimes groups were absorbed in a particular game for days on end, the children running out to carry straight on from where they'd left off the day before; sometimes a group finding itself one short to form two equal teams would dispatch someone to negotiate with another group for an extra member. The nine-year-old and you somehow always tended to be in different groups, and in fact this was still the case when you both were one year older. But because the groups mixed and changed so often, nobody really noticed. But despite normally being in different groups, you always had a good idea of how each other played; while never too close, you were never too far either.

At school all the children were normally with others of the same age, but when everybody came back home and went out into the road, some of them would be asked to take their smaller brothers and sisters. Then everybody would recall how to adjust their play for the little ones, and take turns tapping paper or rubber balloons slowly back and forth. Struck by little hands, the balloons would only float up a short distance before falling back down, and sometimes they'd drift off in unexpected directions. The older children would deftly scoop them up and send them back in a beautiful arc to the hands they'd come from. They simply followed the ways they'd seen other older children behave in the past.

Because the children ranged over three or four school years, there were inevitably considerable differences in height and ability, so the games they played were not normally competitive. Rather than winning or losing, the games would involve taking and swapping roles; their endings would be left to chance. They did have running races for a while, though, at the time of year when everyone was practicing at school for their sports days. The long narrow road was very good for racing, but the children were afraid the adults would put a stop to it: the adults would say that even with only a few passers-by, to have a lot of children running full pelt at the same time would be a dangerous nuisance. Of course, when people were going past, the children normally moved to the side of the road or stopped altogether. They kept their eyes out for people and bicycles in the distance and would guess in advance where they were likely to turn off. If somebody was laughing and trying to dodge their way through the group of children, then they might deliberately get in the person's way. They always thought about how best to react.

To avoid a ban on running they decided to divide into two teams and use rolled-up sheets of paper as batons to pass between successive runners. This way only two children would be running at any one time. In keeping with the practice at their schools they decided everybody should be allotted to the different teams in order of height. But then they thought this would mean that one team was bound to have a slight advantage, so they introduced another stage whereby everybody paired up by height to play rock-paper-scissors. The winner from each pair decided which team to join. When the process had started with the smallest pair, the younger child stood beside you and your partner and muttered, "It wouldn't be fair if we were both on the same team." Your partner readily agreed and said, "Okay, whoever wins we'll make sure you're not."

It's hard to remember whether your team won or lost that day. Both the younger child and you were satisfied. You ran different legs so the arrangement you'd made was not obvious to the other children, and the simple fact that it had been suggested showed that you shared an understanding that you were far and away the fastest runners. This was evident already, both from your status as class team runners at school, and more especially from what had happened recently when you were playing another type of game.

This game too was one for which the long narrow road was well-suited. All but one of the children lined up across the road, while the remaining child took up a position some distance farther down. Facing away from the others the child on its own would count to ten in a loud voice while the others would move quickly and silently down the road. When the child stopped counting and turned around everybody else had to be completely still. Instead of conventional numbers, the counting was based on a rapid chant of ten short syllables, so the most they could take were two or three steps, and toward the start of the game some would take just one. The child who was counting would vary pace when turning around, moving slowly at first to encourage the others to think they might take just one more step, and then speed up to catch them off balance. It was alright for someone to have a leg in the air as long as they didn't wobble. If someone was caught moving, then their name would be called out and they'd have to withdraw. If no one was moving at all, then the child would just turn around and start chanting again.

The end of the game was when somebody managed to touch the child's back. The one who'd done so would then try to run off, and the child who'd been counting would give chase. When caught the "toucher" would take over the role of "counter." This wasn't really a punishment because being the counter was the most enjoyable part of the game—having the stealthy, silent group drawing nearer and nearer when you had your back turned, wondering whether you were about to be touched, the satisfaction of catching others off balance and sending them away.

> *You ran on and on, as though you'd both keep going wherever the road led.*

When somebody touched the counter's back, they were in easy reach of course, so normally the counter would catch the toucher without having to run at all. A toucher who was much more agile than the counter would begin to get away, but changing roles was part of the game, so after a short while, amid the shouts of the hitherto silent children, the toucher would, without making it seem too deliberate, slow down and be caught.

During the game that day, you touched the younger one's back and then ran off very fast, as if you really wanted to get away. Neither of you, nor any of the others, had expected this. But the younger one followed you and in no time you were both well away from the group, going back well past the game's start line. There'd been just one pace between you when you set off, and that one-pace distance was maintained as long as you ran. You ran on and on, as though you'd both keep going wherever the road led.

As soon as it dawned on you that you'd come much too far your pace slackened and your pursuer reached out to touch your shoulder. You both burst out laughing. Yet having always avoided being alone together you now felt awkward, a feeling that you concealed behind efforts to control your breathing. You both turned around toward the distant group and jogged back together side by side.

If you were both the same did that mean the slightly younger, slightly smaller one was faster? Perhaps you'd wanted never to come across such a person. Perhaps you wanted to erase the fact that you had. Perhaps you wanted to erase the person. Or perhaps, looked at from the other side, that person wanted to erase you. You were thinking with every step you ran. But erasing one person wouldn't do it; erasing two or three wouldn't either. To have dashed away like that was to have lost already. Your lungs and legs were still restless, but your thinking was very calm.

This never came back to you during the period when you both exchanged those formal bows; but much later, that noontime in spring, the call reminded you of it, and afterward everything always came back together. Perhaps on that spring day, again, there was someone you wanted to erase.

Translated by Angus Turvill • Japanese | Japan

Born in 1966, CARSTEN RENÉ NIELSEN
is the author of several books of poetry.
His work has been featured in magazines in
Italy, Germany, Canada, and the U.S.
These poems come from his latest collection,
Enogfyrre ting (Forty-One Objects),
published by Ekbátana in 2017.

Støvsuger

Alt har sin oprindelse i døende stjerner: kviksølv og aluminium, blyanter
og stemmegafler, selv jernaber og svævende roser. Alt er stjernestøv tilsat
gravitation, og alt stod som støv i hans stue: et fjernsyn, en sofa, et bord
af støv. Mens fisk af støv gik i opløsning i hans akvarium, gjorde jeg rent i
lejligheden, og da jeg slukkede støvsugeren, kunne jeg høre ham synge inde
i den, en sømandsvise var det vist. I den tomme lejlighed lød det så klart,
som var alt i verden ved at begynde forfra.

Vacuum

Everything has its origin in dying stars: mercury and aluminum, pencils and tuning forks, even iron monkeys and hovering roses. Everything is stardust with added gravitation, and all was made of dust in his living room: a television, a sofa, a table of dust. While fish of dust dissolved in his aquarium, I cleaned the apartment, and when I turned off the vacuum, I could hear him singing from inside it, a sea shanty I think it was. In the empty apartment it sounded so clearly as if everything in the world was about to begin all over again.

Køleskab

Jeg vågnede op inde i mit køleskab og overvejede, om det måske ikke var
på tide at begrænse sit alkoholforbrug. Besluttede ikke desto mindre at
blive siddende lidt for at studere klimaet og lysforholdene. Tænk bare, der
kom en snebyge, og sjældent har jeg set et smukkere tusmørke. Ærter hang
blinkende på nattehimlen, undergrunden var fuld af æg. Som med alt andet
er selv oplevelsen af virkelig skønhed betinget af et vist mådehold, så spørgs-
målet var, om der var nogen, der kunne høre mig. "Kan jeg komme ud nu,"
spurgte jeg tøvende, "kan jeg?"

Refrigerator

I woke up inside my refrigerator and questioned whether it wasn't about time to cut back on my drinking. Decided nevertheless to remain there a bit, studying the climate and the light conditions. But wouldn't you know, there came a snow shower, and rarely have I ever seen a more remarkable twilight. Peas hung twinkling in the night sky, and the ground was full of eggs. Like everything else, the experience of true beauty depends upon a certain moderation, so the question was whether or not someone could hear me. "May I come out now," I asked hesitantly, "May I?"

Translated by David Keplinger • Danish | Denmark

Spejl

Nøgen, let frysende og noget forvirret står han i det overraskende svagt oplyste hinsides sammen med andre nyligt afdøde og ser på en engel, der er ved at barbere sig. Selv om den ikke har et spejlbillede, holder den et barberspejl op og løfter hagen, som den har set mennesker gøre.

Mirror

Naked, slightly cold and somewhat confused, he stands in the surprisingly dim-lit hereafter together with other recently deceased and looks at an angel, who is giving itself a shave. Even though it has no reflection, it holds up a shaving mirror and lifts up the chin, as it has seen humans do.

Translated by David Keplinger • Danish | Denmark

Kogebog

Alt var lavet efter opskrifter i kogebogen *Skygger og støv*. Under forretten summede fluer omkring vores suppe, der var så klar, at det virkede, som om tallerkenerne var tomme. Før hovedretten blev lyset dæmpet, så ingen kunne se, hvad der blev serveret. Det kunne have været pollen, en gas en anelse tungere end luft, liv på andre planeter. Desserten var så luftig, at man ikke kunne nå at løfte sin gaffel op til munden, før stykket på den var forsvundet. Da vi endelig rejste os, lød vores skramlen med stolene som vind i trækroner. Vores afskedsreplikker var blot suk på suk.

Cookbook

Everything was made from recipes in the cookbook *Shadows and Dust*.
During the first course flies buzzed around our soup, which was so clear
that it seemed as if the plates were empty. Before the main course the light
was dimmed, so nobody could see what was served. It could have been
pollen, a gas just slightly heavier than air, life on other planets. The dessert
was so airy, you couldn't raise the fork to your mouth in time, before the
piece on it had disappeared. When we finally left the table, our clattering of
chairs sounded like wind in treetops. Our farewells, only sighs upon sighs.

Translated by David Keplinger • Danish | Denmark

Smalfilm

De døde er altid filmet med en lyssætning på grænsen mellem to årstider. De går rundt med ryggen til under en novembers grå skyer, står som mørke silhuetter blandt nøgne træer i den skarpe forårssol, sidder med torso og ansigt helt i skygge på en af de sidste sommerdage. En sjælden gang er der nogen, der smilende går hen imod kameraet, taler til det. Vi ser læberne bevæge sig, men hører intet. Det varer kun et øjeblik, så klippes der til noget andet: et barn på en strand, så en kvinde i et køkken, en bil der kører på en øde landevej, buske og højt græs der bølger i vinden.

8 mm Film

The dead are always filmed in a lighting that falls between two seasons. They walk around with their backs to us under the gray November clouds, stand as dark silhouettes among naked trees in the bright sun of spring, sit with torso and face completely in the shadows on one of the last summer days. On rare occasions there is someone smiling who moves toward the camera, talks to it. We see the lips move but hear nothing. It only lasts a moment, then it cuts to something else: a child on a beach, then a woman in a kitchen, a car on a deserted country road, bushes and tall grass swaying in the wind.

Translated by David Keplinger • Danish | Denmark

Born in Chile but residing in New York,
CARLOS LABBÉ is a fiction writer, literary
critic, musician, and founding member
of Sangría Editora. The author of nine books
of fiction, he was chosen in 2010 as
one of *Granta*'s Best Young Spanish-
Language Novelists.

Espíritu de escalera

Hay un hombre viviendo en la escalera. Resulta absurdo pensarlo, pero desde el lunes está ahí. Cada mañana, al bajar, me lo he encontrado sentado en el mismo escalón, el cuarto entre el primero y el segundo piso, vestido con la misma amarillenta camisa y un abultado bolso negro a su lado. Permanece mirando la puerta que da a la calle, como a la espera de que en cualquier momento entre el administrador del edificio a gritarle hasta cuándo.

—¿En qué piensas? pregunta Elena, a mi lado. No le respondo. Estoy tirado boca arriba a lo ancho de mi cama, con la vista fija en el pedazo de cielo azul que se ve entre los edificios desde la ventana abierta. Observo las formas de las nubes algodonadas que pasan tranquilamente. Un barco. Una serpiente o un gusano. Una cara gorda soplando. Miro a Elena, que lee un libro de Tintín a pocos centímetros, apoyada su cabeza en el codo de su mano izquierda, y con la derecha da vuelta las páginas cada cierto tiempo. Me levanto, veo qué lee. Lo recuerdo. Tintín regresa a su departamento y se encuentra en la escalera con un tipo que está de pie y le da cuerda a su reloj. Tintín, astuto, sospecha de inmediato. ¿Pero por qué es extraño que alguien escoja la escalera para llevar a cabo alguna costumbre cotidiana?

—Me da un poco de nervio. Es decir, no lo conozco y debiera haberlo visto crecer, me muero de curiosidad pero también siento tanta culpa. Aunque culpa por él, no por mi hermana. ¿Le habrá preguntado alguna vez por mí, o por sus abuelos? Oigo a Elena desde el baño, ordenándose . . .

The Spirit of the Staircase

There's a man living in the stairwell. It's absurd to think it, but he's been there since Monday. Every morning, on my way down, I've run into him, dressed in the same bright yellow shirt, sitting on the landing between the second floor and the first, an enormous black duffel bag at his side. He keeps looking at the door that opens onto the street, as if expecting that at any moment the building super will come in and kick him out.

—What're you thinking? asks Elena, lying beside me. I don't answer. I'm stretched out on my back across the bed, staring up at a patch of blue sky, visible out the window between the tops of two buildings. I can make out shapes in the downy clouds as they drift tranquilly by. A ship. A worm or snake. A fat face blowing. I look over at Elena, just inches away, her head resting in the crook of her left arm, reading a Tintin book, turning the page with her right hand every so often. I get to my feet. It dawns on me what she's reading. I remember the story. Tintin comes home to his apartment and finds a man winding his watch in the stairwell. The shrewd Tintin is immediately suspicious. But what's so surprising about finding someone doing something so ordinary in a stairwell?

—The whole thing makes me a little nervous. I mean, I don't know him and I should have seen him grow up. I'm dying of curiosity, but I feel so bad. Bad for him, not for my sister. Do you think he ever asked about me or about his grandparents? I hear Elena say this from the bathroom, arranging her hair, fixing it with black bobby pins. I'm still on the bed, lying on my side now, my neck supported by a pillow, playing with the small stuffed bunny I found a few days ago in my parent's basement, in a damp cardboard box full of our old toys, my brother's and mine. I see myself going down the stairs, into that basement where I almost never went—even though I lived with my parents for more than twenty years—because it always scared me a little. A line from Georges Perec comes into my mind: "On the stairs pass the furtive shadows of those who once lived in the house."

—And what if it's a girl? Have you considered that your sister's kid might be a girl? I ask her. Elena says no, she doesn't know why, but she's sure that it's a boy, and that he must look like her mother, because her sister, Sofía, looked just like her when she was little. But the father, I say, he must look like his father. A host of associations evoke another paragraph by Perec. I find it in a book I take down from the bookshelf: The piano tuner's grandson is therefore sitting on the stairs waiting for his grandfather. He is wearing short navy-blue cotton trousers and a jerkin of "parachute silk," that is to say sky-blue shiny nylon, with a complement of decorative badges: a pylon giving off four streaks of lightning and concentric circles, the symbol of radiotelegraphy; a pair of compasses, a magnetic compass, and a stopwatch, the supposed symbols respectively of geographers, surveyors, and explorers; the figure 77 written in red letters inside a yellow triangle; the outline of a cobbler mending a heavy mountain boot; a hand refusing a glass of spirits with the legend beneath: *"No thanks, I'm driving."* The little boy is reading a biographical novel about Carel van Loorens entitled *The Emperor's Messenger* in *Le Journal de Tintin*.

—Is my hair a total mess? Elena asks. I don't want my nephew to get all excited thinking he's got a punk for an aunt and then end up disappointed when he's a teenager.

I laugh. Late at night, when nobody is moving through the building, the man in the stairwell must remove a sleeping pad from his black duffel and roll it out across the landing. He takes out pajamas too and an alarm clock set to go off at six in the morning, the time when people begin to appear, so he'll never get caught. Elena drops down on the bed and presses her body against mine. I've got to go in five minutes, she says. We met at a mutual friend's house and met again in a language class. I remember the last day, going down the building's stairs after class, I was a few steps ahead of her,

I wanted to talk to her and I knew she was watching me, from behind, from above. It seems absurd, but I couldn't turn around—the stairs wouldn't let me stop. Months later we ran into each other at a party and she laughed when I told her about it.

—I'll call you Sunday, she says quietly, after kissing me and going out into the hall. The man in the stairwell must be someone who has come home from a trip and discovered that he's lost the key to his apartment and has decided to wait for his wife to come home and let him in. But, while he was gone, she has decided to leave him. The man senses this—it's not normal for his wife not to come home for five days—and he's paralyzed by despair. Or loneliness. In my apartment, I find the stuffed bunny on the bed—the bunny I'd given to Elena so she could give it to her nephew. And she's forgotten to take it with her. I grab the bunny and run to the staircase. Realizing I won't be able to catch her, I lean over the banister, into the space between the stairs, and shout: Elena, wait. I hear her say my name, questioningly, from very far below. For an instant, I see, at the bottom of the spiraling staircase, the trash bin, the pestilent white and black bags. I start quickly down the steps; I'm barefoot and almost lose my balance, the fifth floor, the fourth. At the top of the third floor I stop, distracted by a mechanical sound. Elena must have taken the elevator, I start back up. The final scene in *Vertigo* runs incessantly through my mind, the sequence in which the protagonist pursues the woman up the dark staircase of the bell tower. It strikes me that I've left my apartment door open and I'm overcome by the anxiety of an unavoidable tragedy. On the fifth floor, I see the elevator door open. I find myself face-to-face with the man from the stairwell. He drags his heavy black duffel across the tile floor. He looks at me, his face slack. I keep going up, turning my head to watch what he does next. To my surprise, he removes a ring of keys from his pocket, unlocks a door, and enters an apartment. I arrive at mine, hoping to find Elena. But she's not inside and the stuffed bunny is gone. I go down the stairs, the only other possibility is that she's ascending very slowly, reluctant and uncertain, not knowing if she actually heard my voice; we'll probably meet in the middle, on the third floor, for example. Absurdly I scour the building multiple times top to bottom until I'm out of breath, but Elena is not there.

Translated by Will Vanderhyden • Spanish | Chile

Memorándum

De: José Segovia, guardia de Seguridad
Ciudadana Roja N° 16, Municipalidad de Santiago

A: Dirección de Seguridad e Información,
Municipalidad de Santiago

Aproximadamente a las 10:00 (diez) horas de la mañana de 10/07/2001 (diez de julio de dos mil uno), un sujeto de comportamiento dudoso salió del inmueble público Biblioteca Nacional, caminó hasta la esquina de las calles Huérfanos y Estado, y se detuvo. Vestía como estudiante de educación superior, pero su rostro y gestos no correspondían a aquella tipificación, ya que no poseía barba ni cabello largo. No fumaba ni hablaba en voz alta. No portaba mochila, bolso ni reloj, sin embargo llevaba consigo un cuaderno, un libro y un lápiz. Me comuniqué con Carabineros, quienes confirmaron mi alarma.

De inmediato me dispuse a vigilar su accionar, que paso a describir a continuación:

1. El sujeto caminaba con pausa inadecuada, tratándose de un día hábil en el centro cívico, durante horas de oficina.

2. En ocasiones miraba de manera sospechosa a algunas personas que realizaban actividades normales. Incluso uno o dos individuos se detuvieron y lo increparon verbalmente por su actitud.

3. Posteriormente, a la altura de Huérfanos con Miraflores, el sujeto permaneció quieto durante 15 (quince) minutos, alternando su mirada entre los vehículos que transitaban y las luces del semáforo. Desde mi posición tuve que pedir apoyo al guardia Azul N° 6 (seis) Miguel Espinosa Valdebenito. . .

Memorandum

From: Jose Segovia, Private Security
Red Team N. 16, Municipality of Santiago

To: Director of Security and Information,
Municipality of Santiago

At approximately 10:00 (ten) o'clock, on the morning of 07/10/2001 (July tenth, two thousand and one), a subject of suspicious behavior exited the Biblioteca Nacional, walked to the corner of Huérfanos and Estado, and stopped. He was dressed like a college student, but his face and his expressions did not correspond to that classification; he lacked the beard and the long hair. He was not smoking or speaking loudly. He was not wearing a backpack, bag, or a watch; he did, however, carry a journal, a book, and a pencil. I contacted the police, who verified my suspicion.

Immediately, I was ordered to monitor his activities, described below:

1. The subject was walking with inappropriate slowness for a workday in the city center, during office hours.

2. On several occasions he stared at people going about everyday activities in a suspicious manner. One or two individuals even stopped to verbally reproach him for his attitude.

3. Earlier, at the intersection of Huérfanos and Miraflores, the subject stood motionless for 15 (fifteen) minutes, staring alternately at passing vehicles and the stoplight. From my position, I had to call for backup from Blue Team N. 6 (six) Miguel Espinosa Valdebenito, when I verified that the suspect had been standing there for 13 (thirteen) minutes without moving, in front of a sign on Calle Estado that reads "Antigua Calle del Rey."

Translated by Will Vanderhyden • Spanish | Chile

4. The subject could be a member of one of the illegal networks operating around Plaza de Armas. He patted the head of little girl, approximately 5 (five) years old, who was walking with her mother down Calle Victoria Subercaseaux.

5. Around noon, the subject sat down on a bench on Calle Lastarria and began to write in his notebook.

Attached is a photocopy of the page the subject was writing at the moment I made the arrest, and the original can be found in the court records:

"I'll travel two paths in an attempt to discover something that is in Santiago but that I cannot see. The two paths are lines that intersected in a dream that came to me last night, when I was finally able to fall asleep after thinking and thinking about how to write about the soul of a city. Two paths, two streets that I'll walk down until I come to the heart of my search.

"This first street is the line of time. In the Biblioteca Nacional I read several stories about the history of Santiago: Santiago was founded on February 12, 1541; Santiago became something else after it was destroyed by Michimalonco; Santiago was a shriveled plaza where the broken families of Spaniards living in the south with the Mapuches walked; not one battle of that economic treaty they call Independence took place in Santiago; there was never an armed conflict in Santiago, just the reprisals of Ibañez and Pinochet; in Santiago, first they killed the Nazis youth, then the communists, and finally the poor; the salt trade brought nothing but palaces and misery to Santiago. I know nothing about the city where I was born, the line of time ends for me when I understand that history is not a line, but multiple formless spirals that fade away only to return when one believes they're lost.

"Last night's dream went like this: I was walking through different eras of Santiago, down a single street, until I came across some graffiti I recognized on Calle Lastarria. It was a drawing of two lines, one horizontal and the other vertical, intersecting at one point and continuing onward. The second line, the vertical one, is the line of space. What's known as a synchronic line: I stop on a corner to make inferences about everything I observe around me, the descriptive ideal, the materialist utopia. That's why I brought a Georges Perec book I've never read, *An Attempt at Exhausting a Place in Paris*, in which the Perecquian narrator sits down in a seedy bar to describe everybody that crosses the street and sidewalk in front of him in his little notebook. Of course, in the end—I believe—the narrator must acknowledge his failure: the variations in a place will never be exhausted.

"I'm sitting on a bench on Lastarria. An old man walking his dog just passed in front of me. Every day at noon. A man pedaling a cart of produce is passing by; this must be the path he takes every day en route to Vega Central. A cream-colored drop of oil paint drips off the front of a building that's being remodeled onto one of the paving stones. The charcoal sketch on the sheet of paper of the girl drawing the façade of the Opus Dei church. She's pretty, she has short, dark hair, and her eyes flicker in my direction for a second behind her rectangular, brand-name glasses. Three office workers pass by. One of them enters the movie theater. A man steps on a leaf on the ground and the leaf rustles. A restaurant sign. Cobblestones on the street. A car parking. This is why Perec failed in his attempt, and this is why I won't arrive at the black point where the two lines from my dream intersect. I'd need a lifetime, patience, and more than two eyes to describe everything. I'll only ever see one face—my own—and everyone else will pass by without me ever really being able to describe them. And the silence. And the smog.

"In the dream the black point suddenly turned into a point of light. The intersection of the two lines of the city of Santiago stepped out of time and space. Soul and body, but Santiago is a city, not a human being; it's made up of innumerable bodies and souls. My question—and the reason I can't stop prattling on like an old lady—is about essence. A woman and man kiss in front of me, in Santiago and not in Berlin, not in Cape Verde: Why? The tiny black point expands and now everything seems dark, contaminated, although that is the essence, it's an essence all of us wish we could change. That's why we long for everything outside of Santiago—the country, the beach, Buenos Aires—without having to leave Santiago. Why? In my dream, when I entered that black center point, I melted into something outside time and space, into God, into that which is external and at the same time everywhere, even here inside. The point became white, as white as snow.

"I get it now: maybe it has something to do with the snow of the Andes, there above, a constant presence wherever I am in Santiago. My cousin's friend who came to visit from France said that, for him, Santiago was a point surrounded by mountains. He told me that in France, when they asked him

Translated by Will Vanderhyden • Spanish | Chile

about our city, he was going to say: Everything there tends upward. So then why do I feel so close to the filthy pavement? One step at a time."

The suspect stopped writing and remained seated for 5 (five) hours without carrying out any visible activity, clearly evidencing the abnormality of his behavior. He did not eat or speak to anybody for approximately 8 (eight) hours. On repeated occasions, he invaded the privacy of pedestrians engaged in everyday activities, following them with his eyes for the entire block. When a valet told him off, the subject just went to a different bench, and continued his silent intimidation of the passersby. Before apprehending the criminal, I called the Police, Criminal Investigations, and Private Security Blue, Red, and Special Teams for backup. The potential aggressor became aware of my presence, stopped staring at the sky, and looked at me. I did not have to use my service weapon, because fifteen officers moved in to support me, and we proceeded to make the arrest.

Later, when the unidentified individual was being transferred to the police station, the patrol car ran into the vehicle of a fruit and vegetable vendor. Taking advantage of the confusion, the subject made his escape. At this hour of the evening, the search for him continues without success.

MARIUSZ SZCZYGIEŁ is among Poland's leading authors of reportage. A former television presenter, he is acclaimed for his press features and his books. After *Gottland* came *Do-It-Yourself Paradise*, comparing Polish and Czech attitudes to religion. He cofounded the Institute of Reportage, which trains young reporters.

KARTKA

1.

Długopis spadł mi ze stolika w kawiarni Nowy Świat. Schyliłem się i zobaczyłem, że na podłodze leżą dwie rzeczy: oprócz długopisu w szczelinie między nogą stołu a ścianą leży kartka. Pożółkła i zapisana. Nie była to kartka z zeszytu, raczej z notesu. Po obu stronach ktoś wypisał osoby, ich roczniki (lata trzydzieste) i adresy. Już miałem zwrócić spis kelnerowi (taka kartka pewnie jest dla kogoś ważna), gdyby nie to, że wszystkie zapisane osoby są kobietami, a jedną z nich znam.

Kobiet jest dwadzieścia jeden.

Kartka jest stara, ale nie pognieciona, wygląda, jakby nikt jej nie używał, nie składał, nie rozkładał. Nazwiska wypisane są równo, piórem, i zrobiła to ręka wprawna w pisaniu. Kobiety łączy tylko to, że urodziły się mniej więcej w tym samym czasie.

Dwie z nich wyróżniono. Przy Krystynie P. Z Puławskiej ktoś postawił trzy wykrzykniki, przy Ewie S. z Zalesia Dolnego wykrzyknik, plus i wykrzyknik.

Wśród dwudziestu jeden adresów jest adres, którego nie ma—aleja Stalina 16/33, kartka musi więc pochodzić z pierwszej połowy lat pięćdziesiątych. . . .

A Piece of Paper

1.

My pen falls off the table in the New World café on Nowy Świat Street, central Warsaw. I bend down to pick it up, and see two things lying on the floor; as well as the pen, in the crack between the table leg and the wall, there's a piece of paper—yellow with age and covered in scribble. It's not a page from an exercise book, more like a notebook. On either side somebody has written a list of people's names, with the years of their birth—all in the 1930s, and their addresses. I think it must be important to someone, so I would simply hand it in to the waiter, if not for the fact that all the names on it belong to women, and that one of them is a personal friend of mine.

There are twenty-one names in all.

The piece of paper is old, but not crumpled—it looks as if nobody has ever folded or unfolded it. The names are written neatly, in ink, by a practiced hand that's used to writing. The only thing to connect the women is the fact that they were all born at roughly the same time.

Two of them have been marked out—beside Krystyna P. of Puławska Street someone has put three exclamation marks, and beside Ewa S. from

Lower Zalesie there are an exclamation mark, a plus sign, and then another exclamation mark.

One of the twenty-one addresses hasn't existed for almost sixty years: 16/33 Stalin Avenue, so the list has to date back to the early 1950s.

I call the one I know—it's the writer Hanna Krall.

"I've found you on a list of women's names that aren't numbered or in alphabetical order," I say, and read out the names.

"How strange. I don't recognize a single one of them," replies Hanna. "Have you any idea what it's about?"

"I have a theory, but I don't want to offend you," I say.

"Come on, out with it."

"What if the list was compiled by a man? An inventory of all the women he'd had? That's why they wouldn't have known each other—he was counting on that."

"It sounds logical, but it's out of the question."

"Why?"

"Because only one gentleman has ever had me, and he's away skiing in Val Thorens right now, so he couldn't have lost a piece of paper. It has to be something else—a tailor's list, for instance."

"But what would a tailor need dates of birth for?"

"Hmm, yes, that's a good point."

Hanna Krall

Translated by Antonia Lloyd-Jones • Polish | Poland

2.

The women's surnames seem more likely to be their maiden names, as they must have been in their late teens, or about twenty at the time. Nobody at 28

Londyńska Street has ever heard of Katarzyna S. Perhaps she just rented a room there for a short time? From the lists of tenants in stairwells I identify people with first names that sound out of date—there's a chance they're old enough to remember a neighbor from the early 1950s. I call Franciszeks, Józefs, and Wacławs. There's nothing at 59 Sienna Street. Nothing at 26/6 Mickiewicz Street. And nothing at 8 Dynasy Street.

And five more nothings.

I call Hanna Krall again. "Have you had any new ideas?"

"It could be a doctor's list."

"But why would a doctor have brought a list of patients to the New World café, and why fifty years later?"

3.

I decide to place a small ad in the Warsaw edition of the main daily newspaper. But I can't say I'm looking for some women whose names are on a list I found on the floor. What's more, I (still) have a hunch it was written by a man who didn't want to get his love affairs mixed up.

"I'm writing a feature about the women of Warsaw in the 1950s..." I add the names they could have had at the time, and the streets where they lived.

Next day I get the first call. "My name is Katarzyna Meloch, and you mentioned me in your advertisement."

I glance at the list. "I'm sorry, but you aren't mentioned here at all."

(My profession has taught me that this sort of thing happens—there are people, especially lonely ones, who like to assume other people's stories, as a way of seeking attention.)

"No, you are looking for me. But as Irena Dąbrowska."

"Yes, that's right, I am looking for Irena Dąbrowska."

"That's me. I didn't just change my surname, I changed my first name too. Does that interest you? Perhaps I can tell what the list is all about—let's meet at the café tomorrow."

Irena Przybyłowska

4.

Next day, Katarzyna Meloch is at the New World café.

She's a journalist, author of a book called *An Invitation to Loving*, portraits of writers of the generation that wrote for the biweekly literary journal *Współczesność* (Modern Times) in the 1960s. She's brought a photograph with her.

"Why did you change your first name and your surname?"

"It was in 1968, to do with the situation in March that year. The witch hunt against Jews had started, and lots of people had had their original Jewish names exposed, which they'd changed to Polish ones during the war, for obvious reasons. I'd been called Irena Dąbrowska for the past twenty-eight years, and I thought: This is it, now I have to come clean. I must tell other people the truth, but I must tell myself too—I am a Jew, and my real name is Katarzyna Meloch. I knew I'd feel better as soon as I'd done it."

"And did you?"

"It reached the point where now I'm a member of a society called the

Translated by Antonia Lloyd-Jones • Polish | Poland

*Katarzyna Meloch,
aka Irena Dąbrowska*

Children of the Holocaust, I inspire other people, and you know what? There's always someone coming out of hiding."

"Are there people who don't want to?"

"Yes, and they die of heart attacks."

"Why heart attacks?"

"If a guy is sixty-seven years old, and his wife and children have no idea who he really is, what's he got left? People who conceal something so persistently die of heart attacks."

Katarzyna-Irena forgets her cup of tea—she hasn't drunk a drop of it. She shows me the photo. A handsome young man in wire-rimmed spectacles is resting his head on his hand, beside a girl of incredible beauty. Enlarged a few times, the picture advertised an exhibition called "Photography of Polish Jews" at the Zachęta Gallery.

"That's my mom and her brother—Wanda and Jacek Goldman. There was a phase when I'd walk around the city and see them staring at me from all over the place—from advertising pillars and bookstore displays.

There they were, looking at me, from a time when they didn't yet know of my future existence. They can't have been twenty when it was taken.

"In 1939, when our house near the Prudential was bombed, we moved away to Białystok. My dad, Maks Meloch, who worked for the State Archive, disappeared. Some of my parents' friends escaped from the Germans to the Soviet Union. Mom was a teacher of Latin and Greek, but in Białystok she taught history. She told me the stories out of Kipling's *Jungle Book*, while we sat at home, waiting.

"She knew they'd come for her. When the German picked up her Soviet passport, he said out loud: 'A communist, and naturally a Jew!' 'I'm just a mother,' she replied. They let her get dressed. She left, and was gone from my life forever. I was nine years old at the time."

The waiter is hovering hesitantly. He asks if he should bring a third cup of tea, because the second one has gone cold too. But Katarzyna-Irena has nothing to say on the topic of tea.

"I started being Irena Dąbrowska. I used a dead girl's birth certificate. I was hidden by nuns, the Servants of the Blessed Virgin Mary, in a place called Turkowice outside Lublin. They took care of about two hundred children, among whom during the Nazi occupation there were about thirty Jews."

"So what's this all about?" I ask, pointing at my list.

"They're Jewish girls who were saved under occupation-era names. But watch out."

"Why?"

"It's the tip of the iceberg."

5.

I leave the café and call Hanna Krall.

"It could be yet another list of Jewish women, real names and adopted ones. Lists like that get passed around, so do be careful, Mariusz…"

"I'm always careful what I say."

"I know you are, but they might react with terror. You know what? Best leave that list and those women in peace."

Translated by Antonia Lloyd-Jones • Polish | Poland

6

Alina Krzepkowska (who goes by her husband's surname nowadays) is the only one who still lives at exactly the same address as on the list, in a pre-war tenement house on Tamka Street. She's a handsome-looking woman—tall, erect, and elegant, with her white hair in a bun. The apartment is full of books and pictures painted by her husband. He instantly committed the sights that seduced him in Arab countries to canvas. She used to work in foreign trade, and he is a doctor of engineering. On the coffee table there's a copy of *Nasz Dziennik*, the newspaper favored by right-leaning patriots.

We talk about history.

"So much is being said about September the eleventh that we'll have a paradox soon," my hostess explains. "Under plaques commemorating the Warsaw Uprising, I come across young people who have no idea what it was. Soon we'll have wiped out our own history."

Alina Krzepkowska

"I wonder what someone would write in a farewell letter?" That sort of question gives my interviewee an option—if she doesn't want to talk about herself, she doesn't have to.)

"Could this be a list of Jewish girls who were saved during the war?" I ask.

Instantly she smiles and says: "No."

"Why not?"

"Because I'm not of Jewish descent."

We talk about literature. My hostess says she loves nonfiction. She could never bear made-up stuff.

She examines the list. "Just a moment... I know the lady with three exclamation marks. We studied math and natural sciences together. Krysia was beautiful—blonde with green eyes, incredibly pretty. Though you could tell she'd turn out fat in the future."

"How come?"

"Because she wasn't the type to keep fit. Maybe the exclamation marks are for beauty? It looks as if she lived very near me."

"But who could have written it, and why?"

"Perhaps we got on the wrong side of someone? I never hid my views. Maybe it's a Security Service list? In foreign trade I know I spent my time among agents. Once I was in Budapest for trade talks, and there was a Polish man sitting at the table whom I had never seen before. We all said hello, and he suddenly introduced himself to the clients as Zbigniew Kowalski from the finance department. But I was perfectly well aware that Zbigniew Kowalski, my colleague, had stayed behind at the office and wasn't even on his way to Budapest."

We talk about the tenement house on Tamka. "We've been living here since the liberation. It's a famous building. It even features in a book about a wartime resistance unit called *Against Tanks and Secret Agents*."

From here I go straight to the address of the girl with three exclamation marks.

(My profession has taught me that sometimes it's better not to ask direct questions. I would never ask a woman who has written a farewell letter to her family before an operation: "What did you say in that letter?"—that would give her a chance to avoid answering. Instead I ask: "I wonder what someone would write in a farewell letter?" That sort

Translated by Antonia Lloyd-Jones • Polish | Poland

of question gives my interviewee an option—if she doesn't want to talk about herself, she doesn't have to.)

"Could this be a list of Jewish girls who were saved during the war?" I ask.

Instantly she smiles and says: "No."

"Why not?"

"Because I'm not of Jewish descent."

We talk about literature. My hostess says she loves nonfiction. She could never bear made-up stuff.

She examines the list. "Just a moment... I know the lady with three exclamation marks. We studied math and natural sciences together. Krysia was beautiful—blonde with green eyes, incredibly pretty. Though you could tell she'd turn out fat in the future."

"How come?"

"Because she wasn't the type to keep fit. Maybe the exclamation marks are for beauty? It looks as if she lived very near me."

"But who could have written it, and why?"

"Perhaps we got on the wrong side of someone? I never hid my views. Maybe it's a Security Service list? In foreign trade I know I spent my time among agents. Once I was in Budapest for trade talks, and there was a Polish man sitting at the table whom I had never seen before. We all said hello, and he suddenly introduced himself to the clients as Zbigniew Kowalski from the finance department. But I was perfectly well aware that Zbigniew Kowalski, my colleague, had stayed behind at the office and wasn't even on his way to Budapest."

We talk about the tenement house on Tamka. "We've been living here since the liberation. It's a famous building. It even features in a book about a wartime resistance unit called *Against Tanks and Secret Agents*."

From here I go straight to the address of the girl with three exclamation marks.

7.

Next day, Halina P. from the Solec district calls in response to the advertisement about Warsaw women. I tell her it's actually to do with the list.

"I think I know what that list is about," she says confidently. "It's not something to discuss on the phone, but one thing I can tell you— we girls were terrible in those days. Of course the others are sure to try and avoid the truth. They might even advise you to have nothing to do with it."

8.

There's a call from Hanna Krall. "I think someone must have recognized you from TV and deliberately slipped you that piece of paper. For some reason, they wanted you to write about it. Did you leave your table at the café at all?"

"Yes, I did."

"For as long as it takes to go to the restroom?"

"Longer than that, because I spotted a friend at the other end of the café."

"Well then, someone left it there for you on purpose. But why? Sorry, I've got to go—Tadek Sobolewski is calling." He's a well-known film critic.

An hour later Hanna calls again. "I told Tadek about the list—he knows every movie plot in the world, and he says they planted it on you."

"Hanna, could someone have thought you were a terrible person in those days?" I ask.

"Me? Terrible? I've always been very tactful!"

9.

The terrible woman lives on the second floor on Solec Street. The stairwell smells of urine, but the apartment is neat as a pin. She's retired, and shows me her life's work: four hundred maps from the days when she ran a cartographic publishing company. She's gotten everything ready for my visit: rowanberry vodka, brandy, and cherry liqueur.

"It's a bit early in the day for me," I say, as she sets the crystal shot glasses on the table.

"Never say it's too early for anything," she says. "You'll soon find it's already too late for everything."

Translated by Antonia Lloyd-Jones • Polish | Poland

"Why were you ladies terrible?"

"Show me the list, please... Well yes, I can't remember whose hand-writing it is anymore. If it's the man I'm thinking of, he was high up in the Stalinist days. He could have had that many women. No, he may have had more, and this list is just part of it."

"But what was terrible about you?"

"Shhhh!" the Terrible Woman suddenly hisses, and stiffens in her chair, listening.

"Is it a mouse?" I ask in a whisper.

"No! Shhh! Eight, nine, ten, eleven. All right. Eleven steps is to apart-ment number three."

She calms down, and sinks back into her chair.

"We did some terrible things... Hush! She didn't open the door! Oh, they're going down again! We had a moral revolution. We weren't just interested in sexual experiences. It was a rebellion. Our communism was a rebellion. It was purely to rebel that I joined the Union of Polish Youth in college. We believed our parents had caused that dreadful war. We believed we had to live a different way. As one of my friends says, the Church didn't rule hearts and minds, and there was no AIDS in those days. We weren't thinking of pleasure, we thought it was a new way of life. But the conse-quences were disastrous."

"What consequences?"

"Shhh! Twelve, thirteen, fourteen, fifteen, sixteen... Oh, no—they're going to number six!"

"What consequences?"

"Abortions. We had pregnancies terminated as if we were having teeth pulled. That woman at number three is an awful old cow. So nosey. 'Oh Halina,' she says, 'I can't for the life of me imagine how come you were never married.' 'Because it's better to live alone than with an idiot,' I always say, and she knows I'm talking about her husband."

"Did you have a termination too?"

"Three times. I was madly in love with this blockhead. He had a wife and two children, and I didn't want to cause him trouble. We were together for seventeen years. We went on holiday fourteen times, eight of them to Bulgaria. He told me his wife was a nightmare and that all she cared about was money. And do you know how stupidly it ended? One day, for a joke really, at Christmas I said to him: 'I wish you all the best, and I wish her all the worst.' He didn't speak to me for a whole year! He actually did love her, but he told me he was only with her because of the children. The relationship we had for seventeen years meant nothing to him! My God, it was enough to make me fall to the floor in fits and lie there all day."

Silence.

She's listening again, but there's nothing to count.

"And why are you so stiff? Why haven't you drunk your cherry liqueur? As I was nearing forty, I suddenly wanted to have a baby. With whomever. But no chance. Abortion has terrible consequences, and these days I'm not in favor of it. Show me that list again. It could belong to a gynecologist too, and that's why I don't know these women... You've touched upon something extremely intimate. Don't go looking for these ladies. Shhh!"

"And why do you count the footsteps?"

"Because fourteen would be to me."

10.

A letter comes from Katarzyna-Irena: "Please don't imagine it's a list of lovers. In the 1950s we were far from that sort of thing. We matured late, and we were still virgins, that's for sure. And one more thing: the copy of the list that you gave me has mysteriously disappeared. I'd like to have the whole thing so I can give it some more thought."

11.

I've had a brainstorm.

One of the women on the list is a famous actress. I've been reading the last name as Krystyna Stenkiewicz, but I should have read it as Sienkiewicz.

I call the actress, who is in Katowice right now. "Good God!" she cries down the phone. "Don't tell me—they're all dead except for me. And I suppose I'm only alive because I happen to be in Silesia? Am I the last one on the list? As well as the devil who's been killing them off, is there a guardian angel watching over me?

Translated by Antonia Lloyd-Jones • Polish | Poland

Krystyna Sienkiewicz

"And why did you call in the evening? I won't sleep a wink now. I've never been mixed up in any shady business, but I'll spend the whole night agonizing about it. I was once interrogated by the Security Service. When Bolesław Piasecki's son was kidnapped, the girls and I were at a masked ball. Some time after the boy was murdered, the secret police thought there were clues leading to the ball. Two knights in armor had come along to it, who hadn't raised their visors all evening. We suspected they were murderers. Or secret agents keeping an eye on the ball."

"Or secret agents and murderers all in one," I say.

"Exactly. And I was questioned on whether I knew what the knights really looked like. Maybe the women on the list were at the ball too?"

"No they weren't. Piasecki's son was killed in 1958, and the list dates from the days of Stalin Avenue, so before 1955."

"What's the house number on Stalin Avenue?"

"Sixteen, apartment thirty-three."

"I used to live in that apartment!"

"No, Izabella Prokopp lived there, fourth from last on the list."

"But so did I! In the 1960s. At Izabella's mother's place—she was a famous opera singer between the wars. I rented a room, until I was forced out of it by the Big Blancmange. I had to move out, because she'd settled in for good."

"The big who?"

"The Big Blancmange, but there was a Little Blancmange as well, you know. The Blancmanges had all the appeal of blancmange, and they had bleached hair the color of blancmange too. They came to Warsaw to rub shoulders with the big city. The Big one, whose name was Hania, was the sweetheart of a stage performer. They both danced on the table in the movie *Gangsters and Philanthropists*. I'm a generous person, so I let her stay at my place, until she pushed me out. Those were the days!"

"Beautiful girls everyone dreamed about, and who had great futures ahead of them?"

"But I had nothing to do with any married men, so it can't be a list of lovers. Did you say Irena Przybyłowska from Dziekanka Street is there? She's a close friend of mine, she was very respectable. She went to live in Szydłowiec with her husband who was a vet, and her married name is Hanusz. She graduated in Polish and worked as a high-school teacher. No, it can't be an inventory of love affairs. And terminated pregnancies are right out of the question!"

12.

I try to find evidence of Izabella Prokopp at her mother's apartment, and while I'm at it, of Krystyna Sienkiewicz and the Big Blancmange. I'm helped by a small chain of individuals including four women and one man who live in three of the neighboring tenement houses.

These days Izabella lives in Józefów. She studied musicology. Until December 13, 1981, she worked for the literary weekly *Kultura*, and then for Polish Radio, writing record reviews. She and the composer Tadeusz Baird coauthored a book about him. She's been romantically occupied since the age of fifteen.

"Maybe it's a list of those who attended an inter-faculty lecture, if they were all students?" she guesses.

Translated by Antonia Lloyd-Jones • Polish | Poland

Izabella Prokopp

"I don't think that's possible," I say. "The age range among students is six years. Only people from the same year or contiguous years could have had lectures together."

"Then I can't think what else the list might be."

13.

Period. I've hit a brick wall.

Two of the women on the list, whose families I've found, have passed away.

Who visited the café with this list from all those years ago, and why?

"The culprit always returns to the scene of the crime," says Hanna Krall. "Go to the New World café and sit at the same table. Maybe something will happen."

So off I go, and something does happen. I ask the lady at the desk if anyone has been looking for a lost document.

"Yes, they have! An elderly gentleman who comes here regularly asked a few days ago if anyone had found his souvenir list. If you've got it, please leave it with me."

"No, I'm not going to do that..."

14

A man over seventy comes to the meeting. He's in a herringbone jacket, he's not very tall, fair-haired with a beard. He hasn't even gone gray yet.

"The list was drawn up from the tenth to the twentieth of April 1954," he's happy to explain. "I was a junior doctor, and I inoculated two thousand seven hundred and ninety female students against typhoid. While I was at it, I jotted down the names of the prettiest girls."

"But what for? Did you meet up with them later on?"

"God forbid, I never got to know a single one of them."

"So what did you need the list for?"

Owner of the list, first from left, with friends in the 1950s

"Because I was very shy with women. I was five foot six and weighed two hundred pounds. I decided that if I wasn't married within six months, I'd try courting one of the girls on my list. I'd come and say the inoculation hadn't worked and would have to be done again. After all, love can start like that too."

Translated by Antonia Lloyd-Jones • Polish | Poland

"And did you? Did one of them become your wife?"

"No, I married someone who wasn't on the list. A blonde with a ponytail whom I met outside the health-care finance department when I went to collect my pay."

"Why did you bring the list here?"

"By accident. I was reading an article about the actress Jean Seberg and her husband, the writer Romain Gary, who shot himself in the head because of her. He spent a few years living in Warsaw."

"What does that have to do with the list?"

"I'm a distant cousin of Romain Gary's. Do you know how his book *Promise at Dawn* begins? 'At the age of forty-four I still dream of some essential tenderness...' When I read the article about their marriage it reminded me that somewhere I had a letter from Jean Seberg written in the 1960s, and among my papers I came upon my list of the prettiest girls. Just keeping that list in my diary for a few days cheered me up. And that's all. Then I realized to my horror that I'm such an oaf I'd lost it somewhere."

"And why does this lady have three exclamation marks?"

"Because she was the prettiest of all. I'll never forget her... A blonde with green eyes. Slender, though she may have put on weight by now."

"I found her!"

"And?"

"She won't open the door to anyone, she never goes outside, and she's lost her memory."

"For God's sake, please don't tell me any more about those women!"

ABDELLAH TAÏA was born and grew up in Morocco, then later moved to Paris, where he lives now. Taïa's public proclamation of his homosexuality in 2007 sparked conversations about gay rights in his home country and throughout the Arab world. His own experiences, as well as themes of sexuality, Islam, and immigration, feature prominently in his work.

Barbara Stanwyck
(Ou bien: Un ange à Dallas)

Il faisait déjà nuit en Amérique. Le noir. Le monde en train de s'endormir, de s'évanouir. L'aéroport était presque vide. Silencieux et étrange.

Où suis-je?

Tout cela n'avait aucun sens, aucun goût. Quelque chose manquait. A tout jamais perdu.

Après 11 heures en avion, tous mes repères étaient brouillés et le nom de l'escale, Dallas, ne signifiait soudain plus rien. Dallas? Dallas? Il fallait faire des efforts. Se concentrer. C'est quoi déjà ce nom? Ah, je vois, je vois. La ville où se passait la série de mon enfance: des riches tellement riches, ennuyeux et un peu dégénérés, qui n'ont rien d'autre à faire que de passer leur temps à se trahir et à se faire des guerres tellement inutiles. Mais cela ne suffit pas à combler le vide de leur existence.

Quoi d'autre dans ce nom, dans ce Dallas? Pour fuir ma panique et le sentiment d'étrangeté, je continue de me concentrer. Le titre d'un film, un mélodrame déchirant sur les injustices sociales, me revient à l'esprit. C'est vague. Puis, de plus en plus précis. *Stella Dallas*. Je vois l'héroïne du film. Elle est incarnée par la merveilleuse et souvent impitoyable Barbara Stanwyck. Je m'accroche à elle, au corps petit de cette femme, à son énergie et . . .

Translated by
CHRIS CLARKE AND EMMA RAMADAN

Barbara Stanwyck, or An Angel in Dallas

Night had already fallen over America. Dark. Everyone busy falling asleep, passing out. The airport was almost empty. Silent and strange.

Where am I?

None of it made any sense, had any meaning. Something was missing. Lost forever.

After eleven hours on a plane, all my points of reference were scrambled, and the name of my layover, Dallas, suddenly had no significance. Dallas? Dallas? I had to make an effort. Concentrate. Where do I know that name from again? Oh, I see, I see. The city where the TV series I watched as a child took place: where the rich were so rich and so annoying, degenerates with nothing to do but spend their time betraying each other and waging utterly pointless wars among themselves. But it was never enough to fill the void of their existences.

What else is there in this name, in this Dallas? To flee my panic and my feeling of foreignness, I keep concentrating. The title of a film comes to mind, a harrowing melodrama on social injustice. It's vague. Then, more and more precise. *Stella Dallas*. I can see the film's heroine. She's played by the marvelous and often merciless Barbara Stanwyck.

I cling on to her, to this woman's small body, to her energy, and I begin to dream of her.

Barbara Stanwyck: The Mother of America.

Seated not far from a souvenir shop, I search through the fog in my head for other images of the actress. She alone will help me not to lose myself entirely in this unknown American land which, deep inside me, I feel has been pulled straight out of an old science fiction book. Something isn't quite right here either. So I go toward the actress. I summon her. I call to her. I draw even closer to her.

Barbara. Barbara. Barbara. Barbara Stanwyck... It's like magic. She is here with me now. Truly. I close my eyes and I see her. I bring her back to life and I want to speak to her.

Barbara Stanwyck often played the role of the minx who was completely at home in her skin, the true embodiment of ambition, the charming femme fatale with no morals who stops at nothing when it comes to attaining the American Dream, often through sex. Making a place for herself in the sun without any respect for the rules, completely forgetting the social circumstances she came from.

> *No one wants to own their evil. Everyone lies to themselves, and to us. Not Barbara Stanwyck.*

Her voice awakens within me. Lost as I am in America, she is the soundtrack that reassures me. Everything is already in my head. A soft voice, a bit mocking. Talking a mile a minute. Absolute determination. Something you can't put your finger on. Someone who no longer has time on her side. It's sad, deeply sad. And sometimes, it's tender. I sense a wounded being, cut in two, overrun by agonizing memories: the first tragedy. I listen to a woman forced to transform herself in order to exist. To emigrate. Leave everything behind. Never cry.

In Morocco, where I lived until I was twenty-five, I was only able to see three films starring Barbara Stanwyck, but that was enough to give me an idea of her and her vision of the world. Of America. I recognized myself in the path she marked out: going straight for the goal, never looking back. Not getting caught in the traps of the system and its alienating language. Being stronger and more intelligent than the others, those who don't give you the least bit of thought, neither you nor your destiny. Above all not allowing the clichés to deter you. Just the opposite: without any hesitation, the stereotypes must be pulverized. And, if necessary, never hesitating to play up ambiguity. Giving oneself completely, absolutely not. Never. In this world, no one is worth that, the sacrifice of your self and your skin.

Long before becoming a Hollywood actress and star, Barbara Stanwyck had lived the lives of nearly all the determined and touching characters she would go on to portray on the screen. From one role to the next, she wrote her vision, offering clues about herself, her bisexuality, and the tormented, violent history of the United States.

In *Double Indemnity*, she is completely aligned with evil. Manipulating again and again. Pushing the other to murder, handing him the weapon, giving him the order. Promising to spread her legs for him, later. She is the minx in all her splendor. I'm supposed to hate her, to speak ill of her. The opposite happens. I love her. I am homosexual and I'm in love with her. She's my mother, too. She avenges me for some unknown troubled past. Glued to the TV screen, I wait for her appearance. I learn about life from her. I will do as she does. No one wants to own their evil. Everyone lies to themselves, and to us. Not Barbara Stanwyck. She tells the truth about herself and about America. She is the dim light of this land. She falls. She dies in these films. But each time, it's lived like a triumph. I live it like that. I relive it like that in the Dallas airport. Barbara Stanwyck cannot truly die. That strength cannot dissipate. She is still here. Beside me. Together, we await the next plane.

Four hours to kill in Dallas before my second flight to Salt Lake City. In my mind, the sensation of flying still dominates. Dallas will never be real. Neither will America. It's a film. Soft and violent images. Yesterday as today.

I fall asleep. I wake up. Three hours to go. Time is slow. I get up. I go into the souvenir shop in front of me. It's empty. I do a lap. Nothing interests me. And suddenly, he's there. The angel. An angel who has just arrived from South America. From Mexico? From Colombia? From Paraguay? I have no idea. Deep inside, I know him. He is youthful, very small. He is white, very white. He is strikingly beautiful. He's not from here. And he is sad. My heart tightens. I imagine what he has had to go through to make it this far. To what some people call paradise. The borders. The rejections. The gangs. The

French | Morocco • Translated by Chris Clarke and Emma Ramadan

walls. Hell, literally. All of this is there, visible on his young and tired face. I want to give him all the love I have inside me. I want to speak to him. Hear his voice. Ask him questions. Console him. Buy him a lemonade made from citrus and fresh mint.

He is alone, so alone. The angel. Displaced. Defeated. He's clinging to something. To what? To what dream? He wants to sleep. America, it's not yet what they told him it would be. And the sincerity with which he expresses all of this, without ever opening his mouth, is overwhelming. I have tears in my eyes. I'm struck by him. By the whole of humanity that is united within him. His face. His despair. Not being able to remain closed off.

I go toward him and I want to tell him about Barbara Stanwyck. The disaster that her life was in the beginning, in New York. The force and the determination that followed. And finally, the success, in Los Angeles. To tell him that he can remain just as sincere and use the system to make it. Not to let himself get chewed up. There are other things I want to tell him and give him. More than love. I want to be naked with him. But he seems so young, so small. How old is he?

The vision of the sad angel completely wakes me up. I'm back in reality now. It's still night. Work, again and again. The dollar, the sole religion. Capitalism, the new name of God. It is all suddenly too much. Too much. He isn't made for this brutal world, this angel. He's not in the right place, this angel. He must be saved. Barbara Stanwyck must help me. But to take him where?

I do another lap of the store. I don't have the courage to approach him. I decide to buy something. Anything. A blue I LOVE DALLAS T-shirt. I make my way to the register. The angel picks himself up. He speaks to me. His voice. A child. Words that aren't English. They're Spanish. Does he know that he's in the USA?

I don't understand what he's saying to me. So, I smile. And I smile. And I smile. I don't give up. This is all I have to offer for the moment. My lips that smile and that love him, this angel. My eyes light up in the hopes of conveying a beautiful message. A tender message. Like in the melodramas.

At that moment, images from another Barbara Stanwyck film impose themselves on me. *All I Desire*, directed by Douglas Sirk. She's a mother who returns to her children after having abandoned them to go become an actress in New York. She is still full of crazy love for them, and she wants to give it to them. Despite everything that separated them during her years of absence. She wants to save them. Touch them. Smell them. Kiss them. Make them something to eat. Influence them. True love like a final gesture to keep hope alive for the others. America mercilessly chewed up that mother's dream. She picks herself back up. She returns to her native land to prevent the harsh outside world from swallowing up her own children and filling their heads with false dreams. The film has a happy ending. I cry. I cry. And it's not cynical. Not completely. Not completely.

Barbara Stanwyck comes out of the screen and moves toward the angel. I step aside. I leave it to her. She extends her hand toward his small face and asks him in Spanish what his name is.

He answers: Manolo.

Translated by Chris Clarke and Emma Ramadan • French | Morocco

For MONCHOACHI—a prolific writer in both French and Martinican Creole—language is a site of both play and resistance, a rhizomatic system of becomings, origins, and renewals. As fellow writer Patrick Chamoiseau describes, "[Monchoachi] has completely renewed our vision of the Creole language—the way we read it, practice it, defend it."

De *Partition noire et bleue (Lémistè 2)*

II.

Beltés au vide se bercent

Dans les joncs : tranquillité, fraîcheur,

flegme et rythme.

L'eau monte, vers le ciel pousse la tige,

Corps de la déesse parsemé d'étoiles

Voix du Lointain dans l'eau versent

au vide les beltés se bercent,

Jardin d'ombres et reflets luisant,

plantes, serpents, poissons entres les cornes,

Dans la corne, huile à oindre,

dans la corne, le kaolin,

Rêves peints, fraîcheur

rêves près des sources fraîches,

inépuisables,

aspergés dri dleau,

From *Black and Blue Partition (Lémistè 2)*

II.

Beauties into absence, self-soothe

In the reeds: tranquility, fresheur,

                        phlegm and rhythm.

            The water rises, toward the sky the stem grows,

Body of the goddess star-strewn

In the water, voice of the Distance pours

            into absence, the Beltés self-soothe,

Garden of shadows and reflection's sheen,

            plants, serpents, fish between the horns,

In the horn, oil anointment,

            in the horn, the kaolin,

Painted dreams, fresheur

            dreams astride the coolest springs

            inexhaustible,

            dri dlo doused, water b'witched, ruthless

nourris riz noir,

blancs cauris

Jeunes filles aux doigts effilés,

pourvoyeuses de brume

filles aux longs cils

belles comme l'hirondelle

dans l'eau des marais;

Lianes et oiseaux rizières susurrant sous feuillages:

"Mâle-fimelle, mâle-fimelle," pieds tounen lenvè,

Vaste cours d'eau gayobélé et mare aux pintades,

dessus, reflets lys, lotus,

pagnes raphia,

vase noire des rives

Clapotis dessous oliviers,

bancs argentés sillonnant pâturages,

Lumière gris-verdâtre dans eau glaireuse,

Bois flottants,

rêves flottants,

spirale noyées dans la brume,

Spirales moirées

et contre, la sueur des dieux,

Toujours de derrière submergent, paumes tendues,

pluie quartz et eaux fraiches

images sans bouche,

nourris riz noir

blancs cauris

Et toutes les parures,

eaux futures depuis premier ruissellement,

Et puis les rhombes,

Régir confins et splendeurs,

épaule contre épaule, scander,

concilier souffles;

Mouvements réguliers nageoires et queues palmées,

Quat' saisōnnes pour inspecter confins,

navettes incessantes le long des rigoles,

> fed black rice,
> cowries white

Young girls, fine-fingered
> mist purveyors
> girls with long lashes
> gorgeous as swallows
> in marshwater;
Liana and ricepaddy birds susurussing, foliage-hidden:
"Male-fimelle, male-fimelle," feet tounen lenvè, reverse-turned,
vast gayobélé river and pool full of guinea fowl,
> above, lily reflections, lotus,
> raffia pagnes, finest cloth
> black silt of riverbanks
Lapping at the olive trees,
> silvered benches cross pasturelands,
Gray-greenish light in frothing water,
Floating wood,
> floating dreams,
> spirals drowned in mist,
iridescent spirals
> and counter-versus, the sweat of gods
Submerging, always behind, palms outstretched,
> quartz rain and fresh water
> mouthless pictures,
> fed black rice
> cowries white
And all the trimmings,
> future waters from the first runoff,
And then the turnduns
To preside over far-reaches and riches,
> shoulder to shoulder, to chant,
> To reconcile breaths;
Regular fin movements and fanned tails,
4' saisõnnes to inspect extents,
> incessant to-and-fro along the channels' lengths

Translated by Patricia Hartland • French | Martinique

Branle des quatre lèvres,

      œil tambou entre dans la grotte

      doux bercement de houle,

      et au fond l'afflux,

      somptueux pâturages tout au fond,

Lait, miel, pierres précieuses,

      colonnes sombres aspergées de lait,

La grande barque racle a la rive,

      "colonnes d'attente du passage" ouvertes

Comme ouvertes ce devait en rêve

      par-dessus l'étrave porter le flot,

      Oh ! Joie, *ca*, meīnme.

Four lips moving,

       tambou eye enters the grotto

       gentle swell's rocking, swell's cradling

       and deep within the afflux,

       splendid pastureland bottom-dwelling,

Milk, honey, precious stones,

       milk-anointed columns, somber

The great barge scrapes river's edge,

       "columns of delayed passage" open

Thus open, a dream this must be

       The bow wave overhead, to carry the swell,

Oh! *this* Joy, meīnme.

Translated by Patricia Hartland • French | Martinique

III.

L'albinos aux étangs

L'enfant c'est de l'eau, les jumeaux des oiseaux

Veillant les yeux baissés la demeure colorée de la fille vierge.

Un roseau   à côté du corps

                                        l'herbe éparpillée qui a poussé dans

        l'eau,

Sur la tête, un bouquet de chibowa:

Serpent lové dans la boue du marigot

                cochon sauvage dans les sources vautré, O très Assoiffé

Faune dans les cornes d'antilope une à une souffle

                l'albinos aux étangs souterrains se désaltère:

Eau versée juque déborde des sillons

                détourne les herbages des champs,

Igname bocantée contre nînoufar

Offrande quatre feuilles ègbési

                                        sacrifice du bélier noir.

Peaux noires brillantes, rythmées

                                ongle médian contre coquillage,

Ongle médian contre dos gounouille,

                                ongle médian sur lapeau python,

Roulant hanches,

                chatoient comme miroirs,

Belles choses brillantes entourées de joncs

                        longues mamelles sur l'eau,

Grandeur paisible, beaux arbres à lait,

                        attirent toute la lumière,

Et sur le gué à présent tout le long,

                        front contre front, proue contre proue,

        réunies les deux rives,

                        pieu amarrage planté,

III.

Albino in the pools

Child of water, twins of birds
eyes lowered, veiling the colored abode of the virgin girl.
A reed   beside the body
                         scattered grass grown in water,
On her head, a bouquet of chibowa:

Serpent coiled in the mangrove's mud
          boar in the pooling springs, O Thirst
Faun bedecked in antelope horns   gust one by one
          in underground pools the albino quenches himself:
Water poured to brimming from the furrows
          diverts pastures from fields,
yam smoked against flower-nînoufar
an offering of four egbesi leaves
                         the black ram's sacrifice.

Black skins gleam, rhythmic
                    middle fingernail counter coquillage,
Middle fingernail counter toad's back,
                    middle finger counter python skin,
Rolling hips,
          shimmer like mirrors,
Glowing things circled in bulrush
                    long breasts on the water,
Grandeur, trees full with milk,
          attract all the light,

And now on the ford all along,
                    front counters front, prow counters prow
     the two banks reunited,
                    the mooring stake driven,
                    drifts ferry with its anchoring,

Translated by Patricia Hartland • French | Martinique

dérive bac au mouillage,

Bruissent feuillages touffus contre coques,

contre coques contrechant grelots,

dans le ressac à petits sauts,

mousse blanche jusque soit tarie,

mollement   dégoulinet   contre

coques,

doux clapotis contre coques;

Puis barque tirant le long des rives

vers l'échancrure boréale,

pérégrine dans les replis,

tumulte, tapage dans les enfoncements,

gouvernail aux bassins moelleux,

Avant, par les jumeaux conduite, barboter parmi les roseaux,

pister empreintes oiseaux;

Images montrées des lèvres en fond trous dleau,

comme après rêve-pluie, croissant lune,

Enfant-serpent couvert coiffe,

Et Maîtresse Splendeur dans l'aval étendue,

comme après la mêlée, l'onde,

comme après le désir, la joie.

vegetations swish counter hulls,

        counter hulls counterpoint bells,

        in the backwash in tiny leaps,

        foams white 'til dry,

          half-hearted   trickle   counter

hulls,

        gentle lapping counter hulls;

Then barge pulling along the banks

        peregrine in the folds,

          toward the boreal inlet,

        tumult, ruckus in the recesses,

          rudder in the wet basins,

Before, to splash among the reeds, by the twins conduit,

        to trail marked birds/bird traces;

lips in the deepest holes d'lo, shown,

        so after rain-dream, moon crescent,

Child-serpent headdress-dressed,

And Mistress Splendeur in the downstream stretch,

        so after the fray, the wave,

          so after desire, joy.

Translated by Patricia Hartland • French | Martinique

ANNA KATHARINA HAHN, born in
1970, is among the foremost writers of
her generation. Her novels and short stories
revolve around the conflict between
the pursuit and appreciation of art and the
constraints and humiliations of having
to make money to survive.

Das Kleid meiner Mutter

Wenn ich an das Teppichmesser zurückdenke, weiß ich nur noch, wie erleichtert ich war, dass es so gut in meine Hand passte, ein Werkzeug, praktisch, griffig mit diesen kleinen Rillen an der Seite und dem zarten Knirschen, das es von sich gibt, wenn man die viereckige Klinge herausschiebt. Meine Eltern hatten im Wohnzimmer neuen Teppichboden verlegen lassen, der Bauboom herrschte, alles glänzte vor Optimismus. In der Wohnung roch es stark und betäubend nach Klebstoff und den Zigaretten der Handwerker. Niemand war zu Hause, was mich erstaunte und erleichterte. Im Flur lagen eine übriggebliebene Teppichrolle, ein Meterstab und neben ihm das Messer, nach dem ich mich bückte, während in meinem Kopf wieder und wieder das Freizeichen Deines Telefons nachhallte, dazu die leisen Stimmen hinter Deiner verschlossenen Wohnungstür und über alldem, hell und hoch wie eine Violine über den Wogen des Orchesters, die schneidende Stimme der Lektorin Rosita, als sie sagte: "Verloren? Das Manuskript? Das ist ein Scherz, oder?"

Den Auftrag für *Zwölf Ruinen*—der spanische Titel ist *Kastilisches Kreuzworträtsel*—erhielt ein erfahrener Übersetzer, Esteban Piro, der in Hannover lebt. Er hatte vier Wochen Zeit. Ich schrieb De Ruit aus der Klinik, erhielt aber nie eine Antwort. Stattdessen bekam ich einige Monate nach meiner Rückkehr aus dem Krankenhaus einen Anruf von Rosita, die ich erst gar nicht erkannte, so leise und zurückhaltend klang sie. Sie bat . . .

My Mother's Dress

When I think back on the box cutter, the only thing I remember is how relieved I was that it fit so well in my hand, a tool, practical, easy to handle, with those little grooves on the side and the tender clicking that it makes when you push out the rectangular blade. My parents had had new carpeting put in in the living room, it was the middle of the construction boom, everything was ablaze with optimism. In the apartment it smelled strongly and numbingly of glue and the handymen's cigarettes. No one was home; I was surprised and relieved. In the hallway sat a leftover roll of carpet, a meter stick, and next to it the knife, which I bent to pick up while the ringing of your telephone kept echoing and echoing inside my head, together with the quiet voices behind the closed door to your apartment, and over all of it, bright and high-pitched like a violin over the surging orchestra, the cutting voice of Rosita, the editor, when she said: "Lost? The manuscript? That's a joke, right?"

The commission to translate *Twelve Ruins*—the Spanish title is *Castilian Crossword Puzzle*—went to an experienced translator, Esteban Piro, who lives in Hanover. He had four weeks. I wrote De Ruit from the hospital, but never received an answer. Instead, a few months after my return from the hospital I received a call from Rosita, whose voice I didn't even recognize at first, she sounded so quiet and unassertive. She asked me "to take on De Ruit's next novel," this was the express wish of the author, whose first book of course had become so indescribably successful. They would be happy to engage me again. I was speechless at first, and as a result I didn't answer right away, such that Rosita whispered breathlessly in my ear, saying that in the office of the head of the publishing house, a box cutter was hanging on the wall under glass, accompanied by a short note from Gert De Ruit: "My esteemed Sirs and Madams, please engage Ms. Carmen Salamanca again as the translator of my work into Spanish, so that I won't have to make use of the enclosed tool. Respectfully yours." Besides that, several employees, herself included, had been threatened with strange messages. She too had received a small package, the contents of which filled her with terror. She would prefer not to speak of it, it made her too afraid.

A few weeks later I moved to Berlin to continue my studies in German. My parents took me to the airport. At a kiosk in Barajas I bought the most important Argentinian newspaper, *Clarín*. The front page showed the silhouette of an elegant man with a stiff hat and a trenchcoat in front of the shadowy backdrop of a bombed-out metropolis. In his right hand he held a machine gun, in his left a pen. The headline asked, in red ink: "Germany's Darkest Chronicler—Who Is Gert De Ruit?"

A short time later Eugen Bluthardt called and invited me to visit the publishing house in Stuttgart. "If you're going to translate all his books, you have to know more about this man. There's nobody other than me who can help you there."

So there stood Bluthardt in his hippie outfit at the main train station in Stuttgart and took my travel bag from me with a concerned look at my still-bandaged wrists.

"Ianua Nova Editiones" wasn't exactly centrally located. A tram took us through the ugly suburbs of the state capital. We rode till the last stop: Hedelfingen. I only remember it because Bluthardt was lamenting that this winegrowers' village was being destroyed by casinos, fast food stands, and a giant expressway. The bus drove toward the harbor, crossed a bridge with a broad waterway running under it, placid and brackish: the Neckar, forced into pools and canals, surrounded by cranes, stacks of shipping containers, mountains of scrap metal, and old car parts. From far away these trash heaps looked like untold masses of rusty paper clips hooked together.

We got out at the Ostkai stop. Silently we walked along the edge of a tarred roadway. Every now and then a delivery truck would thunder past.

The road ended suddenly in front of a weedy headland that jutted out into the widening river. A small path led up to the bank.

The handsome ship sat fast and low in the dark water by the bank, a freighter with a rusted brown loading deck, which had carried sand, gravel, and coal, maybe salt too, up and down the Neckar until Bluthardt had bought the scrap heap and had it converted into a house boat. The inscription "Ianua Nova Editiones" could be read in vermilion lettering along the bow, next to it the double-face.

We sat on the foredeck under a sun shade, heard the rumbling of the expressway that ran past, the gurgling and belching of the water, bees buzzing in the rosemary and basil plants growing in old mustard tubs. Eugen served coffee and braided bread. The double-head was printed on the sugar packets.

Bluthardt pushed a plastic chair up against the backs of my knees. "De Ruit has never sat here, so don't go telling yourself any stories. But I've known him since forever now." From a cardboard box he took out letters, postcards, a moldy magazine, the cover adorned with a graphic of a Greek arch. "This is the site of our first meeting. *The Golden Gate*. Monthly magazine for literature and art, 1947. Editor Alfred Döblin. Between Brecht and Ernst Kreuder are three poems by Gert De Ruit.

"My parents owned a pharmacy in Esslingen. It was clear that I would study to be a pharmacist. But even then I had other plans. Read my way through the different epochs—I'd laid out a proper study plan, divided up by author and country. I mostly scored my provisions in antique shops, there you got more for your money. Often I bought old literary magazines. I still remember it like it was yesterday, I was sitting on the train to Tübingen, winter 1976, the heat had gone out, bitter cold. I turned the pages with gloves on and hit upon these three poems. "Praying Mantis," "Nun in the Snow," "Inner Rot." By Gert De Ruit. They were ballads, a form that's not without its risks. But this guy had twisted it into something insane. Crazy, obscene stuff, violent, filled with the most bitter accusations against the previous generation. At one point he's describing German soldiers shooting Ukrainian infants and masses of people being suffocated by car exhaust. But at the same time he rhymes as easily as other people breathe and squeezes every last drop out of the language, playful, artful, at times magnificent.

Translated by Marshall Yarbrough • German | Germany

"I started looking for the author. In *The Golden Gate* only his date of birth was given: 1930, nothing more. In the university library in Tübingen I finally came upon a novel, *Rat Nap*, published by the author himself in the year 1954. It too was excellent. I had never read anything of its kind before, and I was a Schmidtian, that's in the tradition of Arno, of course, not of that pseudo-Catholic slaughterhouse theoretician. I knew Thelen, Benn, the early Grass, but this here—they were all choir boys next to this new guy, who probably wasn't even alive anymore.

"After long searching I discovered that De Ruit had published in various literary magazines until 1953, but then suddenly went quiet, as if a thread had been cut."

Bluthardt continued to hold forth, he talked about the end of his time in school, how he finally became a pharmacist and at the same time never gave up his old plans to start a publishing house, about the idea of bringing literature and the natural sciences together. The Ianua Nova Editiones list is in fact rather formidable. Everything with any distinction in physics, chemistry, and anthropology is on there, from essays by Stephen Hawking and Richard Feynman on up to Gale Boetticher.

But when it came to belles lettres, as a publisher he stuck with classic crime novels, after all they did pay the bills, together with the pharmacy. Never again, he said, had something come into his hands that had the same explosive potential as this De Ruit.

Naturally I tried to outsmart him, often arrived early at the location we'd agreed upon and wandered around for hours beforehand. I never set eyes on him.

By chance, in the mid-eighties, he found a new clue in a novel by Paul Bowles. It was *The Sheltering Sky*, the first edition from 1949. Eyes shining, he pulled out a book carefully wrapped in silk paper, showed me the dedication: "Tangier, Summer 1951. Tenderly to G. De Ruit, my German Angsthase." My eyes got wide, and Eugen Bluthardt grinned in triumph before going on with his story. "I wrote a very scrupulous letter to Tangier and quite quickly received a jeering reply: 'I wondered how much time these so-called efficient Germans would need to take a slight interest in one of their true geniuses.' Bowles explained in the letter that the German had landed on his doorstep 'like a skinny Sebastian Flyte' sometime in the early fifties and had stayed a few months, totally wrecked from his time in the Foreign Legion. He had written like a madman all day long, but then at night destroyed most of it. 'You will never find him if he's not willing to be found because he's completely mad and a far better writer than most of the hacks I've met during my lifetime.' He gave me the number of a P.O. Box in Madrid, and I tried my luck.

"Sure enough, two weeks later I received a postcard.

"Gert De Ruit informed me that he could never meet with me, but if I was willing to assent to exclusively writing letters or speaking by phone, it would be possible for us to work together."

The next hours on deck passed in rifling through postcards filled with miniscule handwriting. Bluthardt read aloud.

"I'll call tomorrow morning at five, be at home."

"Echterdingen airport in exactly one week, arrivals hall, flight 2010 from Madrid. Wait for Hector Venceremos, he's bringing you my drafts."

"Urgently need an advance, leave a suitable amount in small bills at the Brunnenwirt restaurant next to St. Leonard's Church. Password: Mutabor."

Then the publisher showed me manila envelopes, inside them the manuscripts, with small type, corrections in ink on the margins. On top of one was the photo of a pale-skinned woman with platinum blonde hair, black roots showing as long as a finger, and shining teeth between her dark red lips. On the back an explanation: "Nina, stands daily on the corner of Olga and Wagnerstraße, wears lace-up boots. Give her my royalties, plus a tip for playing messenger, she's a good kid. Codeword: I'm not a skinflint. PS: She blows like Aeolus, give it a try sometime."

"He knew my city, that you could tell, because he sent me all over, but it was the same in Heilbronn, Esslingen, and Tübingen. Where he actually came from, he didn't give away, and on the phone he could ape the Älbler dialect just as well as that of the Schwarzwälder or Bodensee-Alemannisch.

"And so the first book came about, *Martin Malterer's End*, a wonderful novel. Afterward we did a book of short stories, *Twelve Ruins*, and finally *Red-Spanish Zone*.

"Naturally I tried to outsmart him, often arrived early at the location we'd agreed upon and wandered around for hours beforehand. I never set eyes on him. He's a clever dog, he probably tipped his informants off weeks

Translated by Marshall Yarbrough • German | Germany

in advance. When I asked about him it was always the same thing: tall, thin, and with sunglasses, talks like somebody from here. When he sent Spaniards, they praised his manner of speaking. He was polite and very generous.

"There were a few times I wanted to give him up. The whole farce simply went too far for me. And you know, hardly anything came of it. Everything was doing alright, more or less, it was just the biggest diva, De Ruit, him nobody wanted. He barely even got reviews. Meanwhile he kept producing like a madman. Which we're benefiting from now. We can fire on all cylinders. They're going totally nuts for him. Take a look, the latest." He fumbled a clipping with the unmistakable font of a large German newspaper out from the mountain of papers. "From the day before yesterday," he mumbled and made an effort to look modest. The headline read: "'You Are an Asshole'— Gert De Ruit's Publisher, Eugen Bluthardt"

X: Mr. Bluthardt, are you happy?

BLUTHARDT: I have believed in this writer since I read his poems and the novel *Rat Nap* in the seventies. Now everybody's rubbing their eyes— how could we miss this guy?—but it was only with *Twelve Ruins*, with the detour into another language, that it clicked. The Spanish woke up first, then all of Latin America, and yeah, now things are really starting to get going, he's got them all by the balls. And you ask if I'm happy! (*laughs loudly, slaps his thigh*)

X: Where is De Ruit located at the moment?

BL.: I believe that he's lived for a long time in Spain, since often he'll sprinkle Spanish words in. But I can't say anything more on the subject.

X: Is it possible you're afraid of your most important author?

BL.: Yes, of course.

X: Why? Because he could go looking for another publisher?

BL.: De Ruit would come to Stuttgart to kill me if I gave away anything more.

X: You're joking!

BL.: No, one doesn't joke about such things. You think so because you've only dealt with paper tigers up to this point. De Ruit is different. After all, you've never spoken with him.

X: Yes, unfortunately. You yourself have conveyed his numerous refusals to me. He's actually threatened to kill you?

BL.: Yes. He's also described to me exactly how he'll do it.

X: Which is?

BL: I can't speak about it.

X: May I be honest? I think that you and your author—who, by the way, I also happen to consider brilliant—are both laughing up your sleeves. This scheme you've pulled together is working fabulously. For one there's this poem, "List of My Victims," which suggests we're dealing with a highly sophisticated murderer! And then there's the thing with the Foreign Legion on top of that. It's too good to be true, Mr. Bluthardt!

BL.: You are an asshole and you don't have a clue. But I can't hold it against you, not at all. You're just as naïve as I was. If only you'd had a phone conversation with him, you would know what I mean. It's like how you imagine a pact with the devil would be: in a word, life-threatening.

X: You're trying to tell me you sold your soul to De Ruit?

BL.: In a certain respect every publisher does this. I threw my lot in with him when no one believed in him. Now the whole world recognizes who they're dealing with. I make excellent money on him. But I will always live in fear of saying the wrong thing. There isn't a single page of correspondence between us, I have to burn everything. Only the texts remain. If he were to find out that I had sold something off, then... (*makes a gesture of his throat being cut*). But that's enough of this. See you next time, I've got things to do (*gets up, finishes his beer standing, slowly walks away*).

I gave him back the newspaper with eyebrows raised. Eugen Bluthardt laughed quietly in his throat. "You can never tell them the whole truth. But he really is scary, Gert is. 'List of My Victims'! When it comes down to it, I don't believe a word he says. And now let's have a toast, to me and you. Because I thought up the idea of the detour through Spanish. *Here's to your Spanish eyes.*"

As the sun went down over the river, which the pink-violet light made to look even more oily and artificial, Bluthardt slid his chair up closer to me with a nice joint he'd rolled. I didn't sleep with him, although the possibility was hanging in the air. Maybe that's why he was so sour on the telephone.

That was the story of Bluthardt; I return now to August 12, '96, and the moment when he hung up and left me standing in my living room in Glebien.

I was offended of course, also unsettled, but all the same I went upstairs into the bedroom in order to change for this unexpected visit. As I was

Translated by Marshall Yarbrough • German | Germany

looking through my clothes I noticed that my hands were shaking, and I sat down on the bed, closed my eyes, heard seagulls crying through the cracked-open window, my own breathing, my heart beating excitedly. The publisher's anger had hurt me, but my pride won out. I felt rewarded and understood.

And so I picked out a green art silk dress with a wide skirt that I had purchased some time earlier from a Polish merchant at the weekly market because it reminded me of a character from a story of De Ruit's—Inez, a young, simple woman from a town outside Madrid who during the civil war falls in love with a German spy, doesn't pick up on his nationality, and each time they meet has him tell her new outlandish stories about his invented homeland, a secret colony on an island in the Baltic Sea inhabited by a Nordic super race, which always devolve into gently portioned-out doses of pornography before he slips the cheap summer dress off her shoulders and sounds her out about the activities of her loyal republican brothers.

I felt honored to be sought out by this great unknown, immensely flattered at having been chosen instead of the loyal publisher. Wasn't I an artist too, didn't I write his entire work afresh in my own language? Wasn't I much closer to him than Eugen Bluthardt, who had only money and nice words to offer? I sheepishly enjoyed my revenge on the publisher for its own sake, even if Bluthardt had never paid me poorly, or relegated me to tiny letters under the book title.

The next thing I remember is an all-too-clear image of myself, pedaling along a flooded country road. With my old bicycle I balanced on the road's shoulder, where the water wasn't as high—yellow-brown puddles, ankle deep.

I managed pretty well, despite the bright green dress, the black rubber boots on my bare feet. A mesh shopping bag hung from the handlebars, my hair was tied in a ponytail, and I plowed through a giant puddle at the fork in the road while the water shot up to the left and right of me, a shower of droplets glittering in the sun that fell on my cheeks, in my hair, on the dress, on the thin striped paper of the bakery bag, which turned gray and transparent and let the yellow, buttery streusel on the square pastries shine out from within.

The two came up to meet me on my garden walk. I only saw the dog at first, who darted toward me, yapping, and then came to a stop in front of me with fir bristling and started barking incessantly, so that I didn't dare take another step forward. It was a large, black Spitz, whose triangular, fox-like face was ringed by a magnificent fur mane. Its bluish brown eyes, its small, bright red tongue, its fangs glistening with saliva, its pricked-up ears shone in the midday sun, while I slowly backed up into the bushes, the bag with the streusel cakes in my hand. The dog stood so close to me that I could smell its fur.

"Quiet, Stromian, quiet!" The dog obeyed instantly. Without turning its head, it went quiet, let me go, and turned to its master, who with long strides was walking across the grass. To me he looked like a large insect: long limbs; a tall, lean body; quick, deliberate movements; but especially the oversized glasses with dark green lenses. He wore tight-fitting leather pants, a gray cotton shirt, and heavy boots that would have fit in well inside a mine. Once he stood before me, he made a hissing noise with his tongue, at which the Spitz stood up at once, trotted over to him, and laid its snout on the dirty tips of the man's boots.

Now he took off the sunglasses, whose wide earpieces folded by themselves when he put them away. Once my fear of the dog had passed, I could direct all my attention toward the owner. A pale face with sharp features, the prominent chin covered in blonde stubble, eyes that stood close together under bushy eyebrows. The irises' blue seemed green-tinted and matte in contrast to the yellowed whites of his eyes and inflamed edges of his eyelids. A handsome mouth with a full lower lip, the upper lip barely visible. The corners of his mouth pointed slightly upwards, as if this insect man laughed often. The nose, sharply bent and narrow, flared its nostrils, and it seemed to me as if both man and dog were taking in my scent at the same time.

I took a step toward the two of them and held out my right hand to shake hands with De Ruit. By now I make this prototypical German gesture completely automatically. But he reached for my arm, turned the wrist upward, and took a close look at my scars, which run like thick white worms along the insides of my wrists; he ran his fingers over them, they felt cool and dry. He nodded, satisfied. "If they hadn't been there, you would've had a problem right now."

Translated by Marshall Yarbrough • German | Germany

パレード *11*

ああ、誰かさん、私を皮膚せよ、扉せよ、骨せよ、
私は大胆してやろう、彗星してやろう、

なので、

そぎ落とされたのだ、

第６３の肉、それはおのれを裏返すことができる、内奥の棘をおもてに、
ウニのような形態に変身して防御することができるのだ、来い捕獲者、頭
からは思さえ放たれる、

第６４の肉、それに取り憑かれた精神の背中には、その肉の影が色鮮やか
な刺青のようにうねるという、

第６５の肉、それはもろく、繊細である、さわるとすぐに壊れてしまうほ

Parade 11

Please, somebody—skin me, door me, bone me
I will chutzpah you and comet you

And then...

The leveling down

The **Sixty-Third Flesh** is able to turn itself inside out. It transforms itself into something like a sea urchin, repositioning its thorns normally located deep inside so that they face outward for protection. Come, come my captor, even thoughts are released from your head.

On the back of the spirit possessed by the **Sixty-Fourth Flesh**, its shadow swells like a brightly colored tattoo.

どだ、いつから殻を失ってしまったのか知る由もないが、かわりに粘液状の言葉の網をはき出して翼のようにひろげる、美しい、そしてその翼を休めるのは、非在の底の軟泥と一体化するそのときだけなのである、

こうして第５９の肉の死は第５４の肉の生であり、第４８の肉の予後は第５１の肉の前駆である、もう過ぎてしまったことだが、

忘れるな、干からびたなまこ、
密猟する胎児たち、真夜中のめだまの身もだえ、

第６６の肉、それはまるで脊椎がないかのようだ、すなわち、ぬるぬると笑みを浮かべて第６７の肉となり、皮膚を切っても血が出ずに第６８の肉となり、過去へ通じるやわらかなドアに変容して第６９の肉となり、ゆるいゼリー状のかさを増やして第７０の肉となる、

ふるえが、痙攣的なふるえが、これらの肉を駆けめぐる、あるいはこれらの肉が、ふるえを、痙攣的なふるえを伝えあっている、

第７１の肉は跳ねる、とてつもなく跳ねる、精神の葉、と呼ばれるようになるその日まで、

第７２の肉、それはほとんど肉らしくない、ほとんど肉としての実質を失っており、ほとんど幻の脚だけで生きている、だがとても優雅な脚だ、性も思考もたぶんそのなかに格納されているのだろう、

第７３の肉は歩哨に立つ、あるいは暴動に向かう、

頭を無頭のように揺らして、おおそうだった、覚えているか、頭を無頭のように揺らして、

ひかり、
喉、

第７４の肉はしぼんでいる、だがその腹部にあいた穴に私が口をつけ、空気を送り込むと、ふたたびふくれるだろう、恋するだろう、

The **Sixty-Fifth Flesh** is extremely small and fragile, so much so that merely touching it will cause it to break. There's no telling when it lost its shell, but in its place, it disgorges a netting of mucoid words which it spreads like wings. How beautiful. The only time it can rest its wings is when it unites with the sludge oozing from the depths of nonbeing.

Thus the death of the **Fifty-Ninth Flesh** is the life of the **Fifty-Fourth**, while the prognosis of the **Forty-Eighth Flesh** is the precursor of the **Fifty-First**, but that's all water under the bridge.

Do not forget—the withered sea slug
The poaching fetuses, and the midnight attraction of squirming

The **Sixty-Sixth Flesh** is literally spineless. It manages to come up with a slippery smile and then takes the place of the **Sixty-Seventh Flesh**. Then it moves on to the position of the **Sixty-Eighth Flesh** without shedding blood despite getting its skin cut. Using a modified version of the door to the past, it advances to the place of the **Sixty-Ninth Flesh**, and then while multiplying the number of gelatinous umbrellas, it takes on the position of the **Seventieth Flesh**.

And then the trembling, the trembling like convulsions, races around this circle of flesh. Or flesh comes into communication with trembling, the convulsion-like trembling.

The **Seventy-First Flesh** bounces around, a tremendous bouncing, which continues ad nauseam until the point it comes to be called the leaf of spirit.

The **Seventy-Second Flesh** is not fleshy at all. It has lost all substance, living only as a pair of phantom legs. But they are an elegant pair of legs, likely holding both sexuality and thought within.

The **Seventy-Third Flesh** stands guard, or is about to instigate a riot.

Shaking its head as if it had none—yes, yes that's it, as if remembering,

Translated by Eric Selland • Japanese | Japan

ペ・ドゥナさま、
ペ・ドゥナさま、

恋するだろう、
いわゆる魂とやらが入って、

shaking one's head as if headless...

Light
Voice

The **Seventy-Fourth Flesh** is deflated... I place my mouth over the hole
open in the abdominal region and feed air into it. Now it will become
swollen again, perhaps fall in love again...

Doona Bae
Doona Bae

May fall in love
As the saying goes, with spirit and so on

Translated by Eric Selland • Japanese | Japan

防柵 *11*
(アヒダヘダツ)

1.鳥が鳥を超えてゆくさえずり

ま
まがもんだいだ
あいだ
あいだがね
アイダヘダツ
さえずり
鳥が鳥を超えてゆくさえずり
あるいは悲鳴
浅い深淵のうえを
髪のようにそよぎ波打つ悲鳴
あるいはめぐらし
ハアハアきれぎれの閾でもある息のめぐらし
あるいは画像
むきだしの元素たちが
微小なヴィーナスのように飛び交う無修正リアルな画像
そのつるつるした
へりに
かすれた文字を彫り刻もうとする
アイダヘダツ
私とはだれ
でしたか

Roadblock 11 (Separation)

1. *Twittering of Birds Which Transcends Birds*

Space

Space is the question

The in-between

The interval

Separation

Twittering

Twittering of birds which transcends birds

Or a shriek

Above a shallow ravine

Waving in the breeze like long hair, a shriek undulating

Or encircling

Encircling of breath, which is also the threshold where breath is cut off

Or an image

The elements laid bare are

An image of the unexpurgated real running rampant like a tiny Venus

Its smooth

Rim carrying

The engraving of roughly drawn letters

Separation

Who was it again?

Who was I supposed to be?

2.ルリリ

ま
まがもんだいだ
あいだ
あいだがね
雪と息
星と瞳
にだってある
空処な
間処な
アハヒヘダツ
紫の律々に
まず柱を起こし
空を環のようにたわめてさ
虫
エクスタシーの虫
走らせるんだ
ルリリ
リリ
連なるささめきの廊という廊が生じたら
うつほ
うつはり
産む巣の都市の始まりだ
集う
景には
オーロラを添え
人の肌めく境はちらせちらせ

2. Lu-li-li

Space
Space is the question
The in-between
The interval
Snow and breath
Star and eye
Have an in-between
Empty place
In-between place
Sepa-ration
In purple rhythms
First prop up a pillar
Then bend the sky like a ring
Insect
Insect of ecstasy
Make it run
Lu-li-li
Li-li
When the corridor called the chain of whispers comes into being
A hollow sound
A beam
It is the city's beginning, city of nesting and procreation
Of gathering...
For scenery
An aurora is thrown in
The boundaries of people's skin are dispersed

Translated by Eric Selland • Japanese | Japan

パレード12

声までとんがってくる、

ヌードな日、

追え、

パレードだ、第７５の肉がみえてくる、それは夜行性で、きみの脳のくらがりを幽鬼のように移動する、そしてきみの夢見の芋虫をさぐりあてると、異様に伸びたかぎ爪を突っ込んでひっかきだし、むしゃむしゃと食べてしまう、

第７６の肉には斑がある、あるいは抹香臭い、あるいは触知しがたい、あるいは渦巻のごときものである、あるいは世界について考えている足指のごときものである、

第７７の肉、それは八つ輪、あるいは六つ輪、そしてぬるぬるした奴が湧くように、陸地を意味する古語をあとに従える、

ゆついはむら、
だったかな、

第７９の肉、それは捕獲されるとその艶のある声だけが切り取られ、本体

Parade 12

Extends even into the voice—

The nude day

Go, follow—give chase

It's another parade. The **Seventy-Fifth Flesh** now comes into view.
It is a nocturnal beast, and moves like a ghost through the
shadows of your brain. When its probing detects a potato bug in your
dreams, it plunges its outlandishly long hooks inside, digs the worm
out, and devours it with pleasure.

The **Seventy-Sixth Flesh** has spots, or has gotten annoyingly preachy,
or is difficult to touch, or is something like a spiral, or perhaps is like a toe
thinking about world affairs.

The **Seventy-Seventh Flesh** has eight rings, or six rings, and
brings with it the classical term for land, in hopes of hatching the slimy
Seventy-Eighth Flesh from there.

Let's see now...what was that line?
The sacred cluster of rocks

Translated by Eric Selland • Japanese | Japan

はそのまま捨てられて、やがて死に絶える、

第80の肉、それは陰茎を思わせる体から大量の粘液の網を出す、あるいはほんとうにただの陰茎かもしれない、

声までとんがってくる、

第81の肉、そのほのかに輝く袋をみっともないと思うきみは、たぶんその第81の肉である、

第82の肉、それは過剰なまでに他の肉を擬態し、たとえば他の肉をきみだとすると、どこからどこまできみそっくりである、

第83の肉、それは雄なのに子供を産む、雌の卵状に夢を頭に受け止めて保護しつづけ、やがて極小の赤ん坊たちを放出するのだ、

性にみちた蝟集、
蝟集にみちた性、

第84の肉、それは巣にひきこもり、巣と一体化している、ならば生涯そうしていればいいものを、存在の蝕の一夜だけ、取り憑かれたようにそこから這いだし、身もだえしながら交尾のダンスに打ち興じる、まったくもってはじけた野郎だ、尼だ、

第85の肉、それはひんまがった格好で暮らし、正体不明の怪しい燐光を帯びている、

いや、すべてに、
いまや強烈な光がさしている、

第86の肉、あるいは病没の耳、第87の肉、あるいは病没の舌、第88の肉、あるいは病没の悪阻、第89の肉、あるいは病没のアウラ、

何が楽しいのか、それらの肉は集団で幽霊のようにゆらゆらと揺れあっている、そしてそれらのすべてに、強烈な光がさしている、

The **Seventy-Ninth Flesh**—when captured, its lustrous voice is cut out and its body discarded, after which it eventually dies.

The **Eightieth Flesh** exudes a net consisting of massive amounts of mucus from its body, which reminds one of a penis, or it may really be just a penis.

Extends even into the voice

The **Eighty-First Flesh**, whose luminous pouch you find to be so undignified, just may in fact be yourself.

The **Eighty-Second Flesh** mimics the others to the extent that it has become excessive. For instance, if one of these others happens to be you, how do we know where you begin and end? Such an uncanny resemblance...

The **Eighty-Third Flesh**—the male of the species gives birth to its young, receiving the egg shapes from the female in a dream, and sheltering them in his head. Then in due course, the tiny babies are discharged.

A crowd overflowing with sexuality
Sexuality overflowing with crowds

The **Eighty-Fourth Flesh** secludes itself in its nest until it becomes one with the nest. Those who have accepted a life like that must be coaxed to spend at least one night of this imperfect existence and crawl out of their hovel as if possessed, indulging themselves in the mating dance, squirming and wriggling. *Sons-of-bitches danced like crazy.*

The **Eighty-Fifth Flesh** lives a twisted life. It displays a mysterious phosphorescence whose true identity is unknown.

Now an intense light shines
On all things

Translated by Eric Selland • Japanese | Japan

第９０の肉にとって、とりわけその泳ぐ魂にとって、一日はきわめて短
い、およそ３時間ほどだ、そのあいだに水銀の弛緩をわがものとする、水
銀の無力をわがものとする、
はじけた野郎だ、

ついにニチリンヒトデ来たれり、

かもしれない、

第９１の肉、それはまさに、ついにニチリンヒトデ来たれり、のようだ、
自在に動く触手とビロードのように柔らかな表皮とで、盲目ながら、どん
な障害物をもなめらかに通り抜けて迫ってくる、

ついにニチリンヒトデ来たれり、
ニチリンヒトデ来たれり、

私たちはその下に圧しつぶされそうになりながら、独自の優雅な逃走線を
描き出す、

追え、

The **Eighty-Sixth Flesh**, or an ear which has died of natural causes; the **Eighty-Seventh Flesh**, or a tongue which has died of natural causes; the **Eighty-Eighth Flesh**, or morning sickness which has died of natural causes; the **Eighty-Ninth Flesh**, or an aura which has died of natural causes.

So what are you calling fun? Like a group of ghosts, these embodiments become wisps of smoke wafting on the breeze, an intense light shining through each one of them.

For the **Ninetieth Flesh**, particularly for its swimming spirit, each day is exceedingly short, perhaps only three hours long. During those few hours it makes the complacency of mercury its own, makes the powerlessness of mercury its own.

Sons-of-bitches danced like crazy

The sun star cometh

...maybe

The **Ninety-First Flesh** is, quite simply, always already the sun star (which) cometh, or so it seems. With tentacles that move at will and an epidermis soft as velvet, though it is blind it closes in, deftly avoiding all manner of obstacles.

At long last the sun star cometh
The sun star cometh

Nearly crushed beneath its weight, we begin to draw our own elegant line of flight.

Go, follow—give chase

防柵12
(鶏頭鶏頭)

鶏頭の

十四五本はあるだろうか

うたが終わり

亜本体われわれ辺へ脱ぐ内奥の風

によって

猶予

のようにゆらぎながら

あるいは猶予がうなぎのようにのたくりその影が

猶予のようにこときれて

死のへり

の冷気

それでも鶏頭の

十四五本はあるだろうか鶏頭の

十四五本はある

だろうか

私はみている十四五本は

あるだろうか病を得て床から這い出すこともできず私は

ただみている十四五本は庭の奥

庭の奥に

妹よ

そこでは光も虫だろう虫も

ゼリーだろう庭の奥に

鶏頭の鶏頭の

十四五本はあるだろうか

むなしくも美しいこの肉体あの肉体そのそよぎの究極の

血のあふれのように

Roadblock 12 (Cockscomb Cockscomb)

Cockscombs—

Must be at least fourteen or fifteen of them

End of song

By way of

The wind deep inside which sheds in our direction, we who are
  pseudo-embodiments

Like a reprieve

Swaying

Or reprieve like an eel wriggling, its shadow

Things cut off, an ending like a reprieve

The chill

At the rim of death

And yet cockscombs—

Must be at least fourteen or fifteen cockscombs

Fourteen or fifteen there are

There must be

Fourteen or fifteen of which I see

There must be, this illness which I have gained, unable to crawl out of
  bed, I

Can only look at these fourteen or fifteen flowers at the far end of the
  garden

Deep in the garden

Oh sister my sister

That light there must be an insect, insects also

Must be gelatin the garden in back

Cockscomb's cockscombs

あるいは文字

毛のような糸のような

あるいはひと

そこではひとも糸だろう糸もゼリー

だろう庭の奥に鶏頭の

ひとひとひと

が撚れてダンスしてけいれんして十四五本は

みている私をみている

亜本体われわれ

妹よ

あるだろうか庭の奥に撚れてダンスして

けいれん

して

Fourteen or fifteen there must be

Empty, vain yet beautiful this flesh, its final breath

Like blood overflowing

Like letters

Like hair like thread

Or people

So people must be threads winding where thread is gelatin

Must be the far end of the garden where cockscombs

Peoplepeoplepeople

Wind in and out like vines, dancing, moving spasmodically

The fourteen flowers I see and am seen

We who are pseudo-embodiments

Oh sister

Does it exist, the winding in and out and dancing in the garden

The movements

Like

Spasms

Translated by Eric Selland • Japanese | Japan

パレード13

追え、
さもなければ追われるハメになるだろう、

ヌードな日、

すべてに強烈な光がさして、
すべてがむきだしだ、

第９２の肉、それはアマデウス器官をもつ、カラヴァッジオ器官と鳳凰器官をもつ、ゆえに、その肉をおもてに、混沌へとその肉を変成させるさまざまな異質な速度が流れ、涙を流し、

流れ、涙を流し、

第９３の肉、それはじれったいほど緩慢に襲いかかる、そのため、友愛の情を示して近づいているようにしかみえない、いや、ほんとうに友愛をもって襲いかかろうとしているのかもしれない、

Parade 13

Go, follow—give chase
Otherwise you yourself will become a fugitive

Nude day

An intense light shines on all things
All is laid bare

The **Ninety-Second Flesh** has an Amadeus organ, a Caravaggio organ, and a phoenix organ, so with this flesh on the outside, a large variety of heterogeneous velocities are channeled through it in order to convert it into primeval chaos...flowing, shedding tears.

Flowing, shedding tears

The **Ninety-Third Flesh** unleashes its attack so slowly it's irritating. Hence you can only see it if you approach with a show of friendliness, or wait, it may actually be launching its attack with a feeling of friendliness.

Translated by Eric Selland • Japanese | Japan

第９４の肉はササと呼ばれる、

おお、そうだった、私は以前そのササの症例を研究したことがあったのだった、私はササ、きみもササ、この奇妙な名において共同の、からだの非常口のようなものはささやく、ひとりでも群れてね、ひとりでも群れたら、抱かれてあげる、月とともにふくらみ、発芽する血と記号の雫、ササきみはササ、ササ私もササ、

第９５の肉、それは花かごである、美しく繊細に編まれた花かごだが、そのなかにひと組のカップルが迷い込むことがある、するともう二度と出られない、カップルは生涯その編み目の影を肌に映しながら、退屈な愛のパラダイスを生きる、

第９６の肉、それはおよそ排泄というものを知らない、恐怖というものを知らない、利子というものを知らない、だが知っている、人形は顔が命ということ、ひとはもともと穴をあけられて生まれたということ、

第９７の肉、それは第２６の肉の回帰である、まいったか、回帰である、したがって名状しがたい、存在という名のゲーム自体を、なにかとんでもない速さで呑み込んでいる、

ゆらぐ動的平衡？

第９８の肉、それもまた回帰である、第１４の肉の、第４９の肉の、あるいはほかの任意の肉の回帰である、

第９９の肉、そう、いまや第９９の肉だ、それはみずからをむきだしにしてボレロを踊るのであるから、するとそのまわりに、ひとつまたひとつと、第１の肉や第５の肉があつまってくるのであるから、第７の肉や第１１の肉や第２３の肉があつまってくるのであるから、第９の肉や第２８の肉や第４１の肉や第５６の肉があつまってくるのであるから、そうして一緒になってボレロを踊る、踊るのであるから、

あるいは暴動ノススメ、
ジャパンにも、
暴動ノススメ、

The **Ninety-Fourth Flesh** is called *sasa*...

I have in fact researched a number of cases of *sasa* in my day—I am *sasa*, you also are *sasa*. With this peculiar name, something like a collective emergency exit of the body begins to whisper. You can gather together even as one, gather together as one and then be made love to for someone, swelling along with the moon, the zero of blood and signs sprouting... *sasa* you are *sasa*, *sasa* I am *sasa*.

The **Ninety-Fifth Flesh** is a flower basket, a beautifully, delicately woven flower basket. Occasionally a couple wanders in, never to return. They are condemned to spend the rest of their lives in a boring love paradise, shadows the shape of the basket's weave projected onto their skin.

The **Ninety-Sixth Flesh** knows nothing of elimination, nor does it know fear. It has no knowledge of interest rates, and yet it knows. That a doll's life depends on its face, and that humans were originally born when a hole opened up.

The **Ninety-Seventh Flesh** is the return of the **Twenty-Sixth Flesh**. Had enough? Yes, the return. Hence it is beyond description—nameless. The game of existence itself is swallowed whole at an outrageous speed.

Is this a kind of shaky dynamic equilibrium?

The **Ninety-Eighth Flesh** is also a recurrence. It is the return of the **Fourteenth Flesh** or the **Forty-Ninth Flesh**, or of some other flesh.

The **Ninety-Ninth Flesh**, yes, now we arrive at the **Ninety-Ninth Flesh**. It bares itself and dances the Bolero. Then around it, one by one the others, the **First Flesh** and the **Fifth Flesh** gather round. Then the **Seventh Flesh**, the **Eleventh Flesh,** and the **Twenty-Third Flesh**...and so the **Ninth Flesh** and the **Twenty-Eighth** and the **Forty-First** and the **Fifty-Sixth** also gather round. Then together they dance the Bolero, dance to the regular rhythms...

Translated by Eric Selland • Japanese | Japan

中心を占める第９９の肉は次第に紅潮し、動きの激しさを増し、陶酔の状態となって、それを周縁の肉にも波及させてゆくが、激しい動きのあまりにというべきだろうか、第９９の肉は、いまや眼にみえない、

良い徴候だ、周縁、プロミネンス、

第１００の肉、それはついにはばたく亡霊であるか、

きらめく鱗翅のように神に好かれて？

良い徴候だ、口辺は痕跡にすぎない、真昼の皮膚のかけらが飛び立つ、

こうして第１０１の肉、パレードだ、

追え、

Or a call to riot
In *Japan* also
A call to riot

The **Ninety-Ninth Flesh**, which occupies the center, begins to blush, and
increases the intensity of its movement. Its state of rapture spreads to the
flesh on the periphery and its movements intensify further until it is no
longer visible to the naked eye.

It is a good sign, the periphery, a prominence

The **One-Hundredth Flesh**—at long last, flapping its wings, becomes a
    disembodied spirit.
The gods seem to have taken a liking to it, like a glistening lepidopteran.

It is a good sign, around the mouth a mere trace, a fragment of midday
    skin takes wing.

And with this the **Hundred-and-First Flesh** makes its entry—it's a
    parade...

Go, follow—give chase

Translated by Eric Selland • Japanese | Japan

JOHANNE LYKKE HOLM lives
in Copenhagen, where she runs the writing
workshop "Hekseskolan" (Witch School)
with the author Olga Ravn. She also works as
a translator from Danish and German
into Swedish. *The Night before This Day* is her
debut.

Natten Som Föregick Denna Dag

Det är en fruktansvärd sak att vara ett barn. Man står på rad tillsammans
med djuren, grödorna och maskinerna. Man öppnar sin mun och talar. Man
hör de vuxna säga: *Det kommer något ur barnmunnen. Omöjligt att veta vad.*

Translated by
SASKIA VOGEL

The Night before This Day

It's a terrible thing to be a child. You stand in line with the animals, the crops, and the machines. You open your mouth and speak. You hear the adults say: *Something's coming out of that child-mouth. Impossible to know what.*

I see Ma on the other side of the room. She's wearing her glasses and her white underwear. They're made of cotton but look like silk. The nightlight illuminates her cheeks, which are bright fruits or planets, the globes of the face, the face's hanging plums. Autumn is spread across the garden like a saddle pad on a horse. I look at Ma's face. She's looking in another direction. Into the wall or through it. Ma's eyelids. Ma's hands. Ma's glossy braid. She smells dry and sweet like a person. She turns her head. She looks at me or through me. Ghost-eyes. I turn away and my gaze catches in the wallpaper. A shepherd walks through the forest. A shepherd walks through the forest, singing softly to his lambs. Ma reads aloud from the diary she kept as a child. *Girls, listen.* Cosima shuts her black eyes. Eyelids gleaming in the lamplight. Her oiled body. Primrose or almond. Ma reads: *I walk through the house with a weight around my neck. It's a globe I drag behind me. I tear at my face with sharp things: a file in my jacket, my nails. My face is hard as antique marble. People see me and their bodies shake. I speak only of the things that cause anxiety. Remember, girls, I was but a child when I wrote this.* We look up. Holding our things. Cosima's needlework. My needlework. A window flies open and night tumbles in. We open our mouths. Drink too much rain, and you get sick. I don't know if it's true, but I've heard it said. Ma reads: *I speak only of things that cause anxiety. Trains without windows, unhappy runaway horses. As soon as I get hold of pictures, I show them. Hungry animals in dirty barns. Rotting meat. Cheeses being eaten by maggots or dogs. The young, soft hands of dead soldiers. My tongue is pressed to the roof of my mouth, every night and every morning. If someone hits me or so much as thinks about hitting me, I can be quick to sink in my white teeth. Listen, girls. The winds of change are sweeping across the blue mountains. I bit a governess hard in the cheek. I was an outstanding girl. I wore violet clothes or nothing at all. I would write in my diary: Death to them all! I spit on my mother's forehead and nothing happened. There has never been a girl like me. In no place and no time. The ground beneath my tennis shoes was proud and happy. I remember looking at myself in the mirror and thinking: It's a burden to be born to this.*

The night before this day I dreamed my pupils were teeth. A dream vision depicting a table with plates made of aluminum. There lay the dentine. There lay connective tissue and tooth pulp. In my eye were four real molars in each half of my jaw. I had an eye in my mouth, too. It felt soft and alive, I didn't want to spit it out or swallow it. An overhead bulb lit up and the teeth sparked in the electric light. The room was tiled from floor to ceiling. Everything was covered with a light blue film. I walked through the room. Lightning flashed in my mouth and I opened wide.

Translated by Saskia Vogel • Swedish | Sweden

I woke up with a terrible pain in the part of my mouth where nothing has grown before. With my tongue I could feel a small mountain peak. Farewell, my virgin flesh. It's budding time for teeth. When all else dies, they begin to live. I draw a picture where a girl has teeth instead of pupils. I draw a picture where a hand is holding out a fang. Now I'm looking for tools in drawers. Tongs or a knife. This evil tooth shall be torn from my body, so that I, with my own hands, can throw it in the fire or to the dogs.

Today I woke up with a book under my cheek. Today I've pressed my cheek to Cosima's forehead. It's early morning and misty. The window was open in the night. A cold wind blew through the nursery. If someone wanted to kidnap us, it would be easy. Here, all the doors are open. There is condensation on the mirror and on Cosima. Ma turns up in the doorway, and says: *Children, you'll catch cold*. I'm freezing. I shut my eyes and imagine I'm wrapped in a large fur. A woman who shot and slaughtered a bear, turned it into a pelt. Teeth and jewelry.

Translated by Saskia Vogel • Swedish | Sweden

I hear Cosima singing in the kitchen. Coffee and bread. Those eternal pre-served fruits of hers.

The night before this day the tooth ached. It gave off a smell like death or moss. It was a barbarous night. I cooled my cheeks with salve and left my mouth open. Now the pillows smell of camphor and sweat. I know that day was longer than the others. An hour lasted an eternity. In my blood, the weeks and months flowed by. I dreamed the same dream: a mountain face suddenly razed. Clouds resembling dogs. Tobacco smoke flowing and flowing. Ma says: *First this great pain, then adulthood.* Now I'm sitting in the window frame. Ma wrapped an onion compress around my head. I look at Cosima moving through the garden. Her mouth glistens. Glossy stones in the middle of her face. When she laughs, all the white, it blinds you. That needles me to death.

Translated by Saskia Vogel • Swedish | Sweden

Today I fainted. Today everything went black before my eyes. Today I crashed to the floor like a vase. I have been a girl who has passed out on a rug. I know my head sank through the floor. I was powerless. My head bent backward like a horse's in a halter. My braids were reins. It was so quiet and dark. I heard someone coming. Ma calling: *Cosima, come.* Cosima's hurried steps through the house. The smell of patent leather shoes. I know they dragged my body through every room. Four hands I recognized. I wanted to say: *No.* The cramp in my tongue spread to my throat and chest. For a moment I thought my heart would stop. Feet hitting the floorboards. It wasn't my body, it was a piece of furniture. My knee got scratched on a threshold. I thought: *I suppose I'm dying now.* I walked right into a perilous dark. I was sweating and writhing. Around my head, insects buzzed. A thousand horse hooves galloped over cliffs. I recognized this: Ma's scent. Her soft hands against my wet cheeks. Her cool cloths on my forehead.

When I woke up Cosima was sitting on me. She was laughing. I knew then that she was a cruel person. She showed me the book about illness. She told me about trips to take the Alpine air. She said: *They travel through the world together to save themselves from downfall or death.* Pictures depicting sick girls and their stained lungs. Small nurses swaddling them in blankets and sheets. The sky was high and blue. The doctor arrived daily with his bag. He tucked them into furs. He told them about the world and handed out newspapers, three weeks old. His polished instruments sparkled in the sun. You could tell he polished them often or that a nurse did. He had long, white fingers. He reached for the girls with hooks and tools. He had a dirty soul. You could tell by his face and dress that he was deranged. On the horizon there was skiing. Young people in powder snow. Their large red lungs reaching for the mountains. The sweaters and the new ski boots. You couldn't get there with your hands or your thoughts. You sat in your lounge chair and examined the objects in a box you found. Old beautiful fabric. An amulet with a picture of a brother or a pet. A piece of paper bearing the words: *Flowers and skin*. You wanted to reach out and touch the snow, but couldn't. You had to ask the nurse to fetch a fistful on a chilled platter. You closed your eyes and saw: Girls in sunglasses. Looking around. Singing songs in rounds, moving in unison. Long mountain ranges tying countries together, same river, different names. Cosima who said: *Sick people spend their entire lives with a thermometer in their mouths.* In my mind: Chocolate bars in green tin foil. A postcard of dead girls in white robes.

Translated by Saskia Vogel • Swedish | Sweden

The curtains in the nursery suddenly come alive. A wet mouth emerges from the fabric. Is someone there behind it, breathing.

There is no joy in this world. I ask Cosima to fetch lemon water and she does.

Translated by Saskia Vogel • Swedish | Sweden

I know all people must experience long hours of illness. I'm lying in bed. I'm watching my body swell. The fever gathers water where it can. My calves. My hips. Repulsive sacks of water. Inside me my molars flash. I ask Ma: *What kind of a dwarf house is this? My head knocked the ceiling, my skeleton*. She puts her hand to my forehead. *My child*. In the dream my brain appears as a seven-story building. Stone floors painted in brown and pink. The mother of the house, the daughter. I shout: *What is this*. It is a large and practical construction. I walk through the house and see myself in all the rooms. In the kitchen my name is on all the preserves. In the bathroom, my braids hang from the ceiling. A wallpaper in the classroom with ballerinas who have my face. On the slate, a close-up of my sick mouth. Someone teaching a class. Diligent hands raised and waving. Someone saying: *Behold, the girl-mouth. So vile and rotten*.

You were an ugly child from the start, says Ma. *An ugly baby born cruel.*

Translated by Saskia Vogel • Swedish | Sweden

There's proof that Ma was once a child. Her clothes are in a chest in the cellar. I open it sometimes. Hold my breath until I black out. Peering down into the child's grave. Violet, moldering fabrics. Shoes from another time. A black lock of hair in a small bag. There's no chance I'll sleep tonight. It's dark in the house and in the garden. Cosima's breathing. At the foot of my bed is the window. Sometimes I stare out into the night and wait for something to become visible. That nightmare where someone with an awful face is climbing up the façade. I'm under the blanket with matches. I can be here. I read the book about the garden that starts outside the nursery window. Here lies the given place for the oldest and most natural of hunting techniques. A stuffed goshawk can be used as bait, like almost any stuffed owl can be. I make notes in the margins. Cats, minks, and other small predators are caught in box-like traps and used as bait for larger predators. Kestrels or Caspian tigers. An evil monster you thought was dead.

Something catastrophic is happening in my brain. I tried to write a poem about the dog. I wrote THE DOG. Then I didn't write anything else, because my brain refused to stop shrieking: *One or more dogs? One or more dogs?*

Translated by Saskia Vogel • Swedish | Sweden

In the morning light Cosima looks like a person from a holy place. Her head could adorn temples and barns. She's the little patron saint of deer. I don't fear my sister. All that frightens me is eternity and the wet smell of moss that comes with it. I imagine having sunken into a mire. My skin sucks up the green mud. My lungs can breathe water. Climbing plants gather around my forehead. There is no big difference between humans and crops. I too am a mushroom. Ma talks about her time at the edge of the world. She greeted the deer and they greeted her. I ask with my child-voice: *What about the wild boar*. Ma's eyes. I turn to Cosima. I know that she has calf skin on her face. She paints her nails. She has bottles of polish. She has small jars of fat and oil. Lanolin and red pigment. She says: *The magical properties of primrose. The power of rosehip*. She has a bowl with marmalade on the vanity, black cherry.

I am not a happy person.

Translated by Saskia Vogel • Swedish | Sweden

Contributors

NEIL ANDERSON is a teacher and translator living in Savannah, Georgia. His translations of Galician poetry have appeared in journals such as *M–Dash*, *Asymptote*, *Drunken Boat*, *Pleiades*, *The Literary Review*, *Circumference*, and *Waxwing*.

CHRIS CLARKE was raised in Western Canada, and currently lives in Paris, France. His translations include work by Raymond Queneau (New Directions) and Pierre Mac Orlan (Wakefield Press), among others. He was awarded a PEN/Heim Translation Fund grant in 2016 for his translation of Marcel Schwob's *Imaginary Lives* (Wakefield Press, March 2018). His translation of Nobel Prize winner Patrick Modiano's *In the Café of Lost Youth* (NYRB Classics) was shortlisted for the 2016 French-American Foundation Translation Prize. Chris is a PhD candidate in French at the Graduate Center (CUNY) in New York.

ANI GJIKA is an Albanian-born writer, literary translator, and author of *Bread on Running Waters* (2013), a finalist for the Anthony Hecht Poetry Prize and May Sarton New Hampshire Book Prize. She's the recipient of an NEA fellowship and a Robert Pinsky Global fellowship. Her translation of Luljeta Lleshanaku's *Negative Space* is due in 2018 from Bloodaxe in the UK and New Directions in the US.

PATRICIA HARTLAND is a candidate for the MFA in Poetry at the University of Notre Dame, and a recent graduate of the Iowa Translation Workshop. She translates from French, Martinican Creole, and Hindi, with a special interest in Caribbean literature. Her translations of prose, poetry, and theater have appeared in *Asymptote*, *Circumference*, *Drunken Boat*, and elsewhere.

KATHLEEN HEIL is a dancer, writer, and translator of poetry and prose. Her work appears in the *New Yorker*, *Threepenny Review*, the *Brooklyn Rail*, *Five Points*, *Beloit Poetry Journal*, *Green Mountains Review*, and many other journals. A recipient of fellowships from the NEA and the Sturgis Foundation, among others, she lives and works in Berlin. More at kathleenheil.net.

DAVID KEPLINGER is the author of five collections of poetry, most recently *Another City* (Milkweed, 2018). His collaborative translations with the German poet Jan Wagner, *The Art of Topiary*, were published by Milkweed in 2017. With the Danish poet Carsten René Nielsen, Keplinger has translated *World Cut Out with Crooked Scissors* (New Issues, 2007) and *House Inspections* (BOA, 2011). Keplinger has won the T. S. Eliot Prize, the Colorado Book Award, the Cavafy Prize, and other honors, and he has received NEA fellowships in both Literature and Literary Translation. He teaches in the MFA Program at American University in Washington, DC.

ANTONIA LLOYD-JONES is a prize-winning translator of Polish literature. She has translated works by many of Poland's leading contemporary novelists, including Paweł Huelle and Jacek Dehnel, and authors of reportage including Mariusz Szczygieł and Wojciech Jagielski. She also translates crime fiction by Zygmunt Miłoszewski, poetry, essays, and children's books. Her translation of *Gottland* by Mariusz Szczygieł—a candid portrait of the Czechs—was published by Melville House in 2014.

EMMA RAMADAN is a literary translator based in Providence, Rhode Island, where she is opening Riffraff, a bookstore and bar. She is the recipient of a PEN/Heim Translation Fund grant, an NEA Translation Fellowship, and a Fulbright in Morocco. Her translations include Anne Garréta's *Sphinx* and *Not One Day* (Deep Vellum), Fouad Laroui's *The Curious Case of Dassoukine's Trousers* (Deep Vellum), Anne Parian's *Monospace* (La Presse/Fence Books), and Frédéric Forte's *33 Flat Sonnets* (Mindmade Books). Her forthcoming translations include Virginie Despentes's *Pretty Things* (Feminist Press), Delphine Minoui's *I'm Writing You From Tehran* (FSG), and Marcus Malte's *The Boy* (Restless Books).

ERIC SELLAND is the author of *Beethoven's Dream* and *Arc Tangent* (both on Isobar Press, Tokyo). His translation of *The Guest Cat*, a novel by Takashi Hiraide, was on the *New York Times* best-seller list in February of 2014. He is currently editing an anthology of Japanese Modernist and avant-garde poetry with poet and translator Sawako Nakayasu. Eric currently lives in Tokyo where he works as a translator of economic reports.

ANTONY SHUGAAR is a translator and writer. Among his recent translations are winners of the Italian Strega Prize, for 2011 (*Story of My People*, Edoardo Nesi, Other Press), 2013 (*Resistance Is Futile*, Walter Siti, Rizzoli), 2015 (*Ferocity*, Nicola Lagioia, Europa), and 2016 (*The Catholic School*, Edoardo Albinati). He translated two books by Primo Levi for the Norton Complete Works (2015): *Other People's Trades* and *If Not Now, When?* He was shortlisted for the 2016 PEN Translation Prize for Viola Di Grado's *Hollow Heart*. He has translated extensively from the French and the Italian for the *New York Review of Books* and the *New York Times*. He translates screenplays, and translated six of the ten episodes of the first season of Paolo Sorrentino's *The Young Pope*.

ANGUS TURVILL is an award-winning translator of Japanese. His work ranges from the poetry of Kiwao Nomura to *Tales from a Mountain Cave* by humorist and anti-militarist Hisashi Inoue and *The Art of Discarding* by decluttering guru Nagisa Tatsumi. He is the translator and editor of *Heaven's Wind*, a new dual-language anthology of Japanese women's writing. For Two Lines Press he has recently translated *Lion Cross Point* by Masatsugu Ono. He teaches translation courses at Durham University in the UK.

WILL VANDERHYDEN is a translator of Spanish-language literature. His translations include two novels by the Chilean writer Carlos Labbé, *Navidad & Matanza* (2014) and *Loquela* (2015). In 2015, he received an NEA Translation Fellowship and Lannan Foundation Residency for his translation of *The Invented Part* by Rodrigo Fresán, which was published in May 2017 by Open Letter Books.

SASKIA VOGEL is from Los Angeles and lives in Berlin, where she works as a writer and Swedish-to-English literary translator. Her debut novel, *I Am a Pornographer*, will be published in 2019 by Dialogue Books/Little, Brown UK, Mondial in Sweden, and Alpha Decay in Spain. She has written on power and sexuality for publications such as *Granta*, the *White Review*, and the *Offing*. Her translations include works by Karolina Ramqvist, Lina Wolff, and Lena Andersson.

MARSHALL YARBROUGH's translations from German include novels by Marc Elsberg and Charlotte Link. A translation of Michael Ende's *The Prison of Freedom* is forthcoming, along with a co-translation of Gregor von Rezzori's *The Death of My Brother Abel*, the latter to be published by New York Review Books. Yarbrough's translations and criticism have appeared in N+1, the *Brooklyn Rail*—where he is assistant music editor—and elsewhere. He lives in New York City.

Credits

HAHN, ANNA KATHARINA. In *Das Kleid meiner Mutter*. Berlin: Suhrkamp, 2016.

HOLM, JOHANNE LYKKE. In *Natten som föregick denna dag*. Stockholm: Albert Bonniers Förlag, 2017. Printed with permission from the author. All rights reserved.

KURODA, NATSUKO. "Michi no koe" in *GRANTA JAPAN with Waseda Bungaku* 02. Tokyo: Hayakawa Publishing, 2015. Printed with permission from the author. All rights reserved.

LABBÉ, CARLOS. "Espíritu de escalera" and "Memorándum" in *Caracteres blancos*. Cáceres: Periférica, 2011.

LLESHANAKU, LULJETA. "Pothuajse Dje" in *Pothuajse Dje*. Tiranë: OMBRA GVG, 2012. "Qytetet" and "Po afrohet" in *Homo Antarcticus*. Tiranë: OMBRA GVG, 2015.

MONCHOACHI. "Beltés au vide se percent" and "L'albinos aux étangs" in *Partition noire et bleue (Lémistè 2)*. Bussy-le-Repos: Éditions Obsidiane, 2015.

NIELSEN, CARSTEN RENÉ. "Støvsuger," "Køleskab," "Spejl," "Kogebog," and "Smalfilm" in *Enogfyrre ting*. Aarhus, Denmark: Ekbátana, 2017.

NOMURA, KIWAO. "Parēdo 11," "Bōsaku 11 (Aida e Datsu)," "Parēdo 12," "Bōsaku 12 (Keitō Keitō)," and "Parēdo 13" in *Nūdo na Hi*. Tokyo: Shichosha, 2011.

PICCOLO, FRANCESCO. In *Il desiderio di essere come tutti*. Turin: Giulio Einaudi Editore, 2013.

PICHEL, LUZ. "Poema prólogo," "É mediodía," "Coidar os pementos," and "O que se ve mirando" in *Cativa en su lughar/Casa pechada*. Madrid: Progresele, 2013.

PRON, PATRICIO. "La historia del cazador y del oso #1" and "La historia del cazador y del oso #4" in *El mundo sin las personas que lo afean y lo arruinan.* Barcelona: Random House Mondadori, 2010.

SZCZYGIEŁ, MARIUSZ. "KARTKA" in *Kaprysik, Damskie Historie*. Warsaw: Agora SA, 2010. Photo of Krystyna Sienkiewicz by Zofia Nasierowska; printed with permission from Reporter Agencja Fotograficzna. Photo of Hanna Krall by Erazm Ciołek / © A. Ciołek.

TAÏA, ABDELLAH. "Barbara Stanwyck (Ou bien: Un ange à Dallas)." Previously unpublished.

Index by Language